HER HIGHLAND FLING

Also by Jennifer McQuiston

Moonlight on My Mind
Summer Is for Lovers
What Happens in Scotland

Coming Soon
Diary of an Accidental Wallflower

HER HIGHLAND FLING

A Novella

JENNIFER MCQUISTON

AVONIMPULSE

An Imprint of HarperCollinsPublishers

Excerpt from *Diary of an Accidental Wallflower* copyright © 2015 by Jennifer McQuiston.

Excerpt from *Holding Holly* copyright © 2014 by Julie Revell Benjamin.

Excerpt from *It's a Wonderful Fireman* copyright © 2014 by Jennifer Bernard.

Excerpt from *Once Upon a Highland Christmas* copyright © 2014 by Lecia Cotton Cornwall.

Excerpt from *Running Hot* copyright © 2014 by HelenKay Dimon.

Excerpt from *Sinful Rewards 1* copyright © 2014 by Cynthia Sax.

Excerpt from *Return to Clan Sinclair* copyright © 2014 by Karen Ranney LLC.

Excerpt from *Return of the Bad Girl* copyright © 2014 by Codi Gary.

EPub Edition JANUARY 2015 ISBN: 9780062387226

Print Edition ISBN: 9780062387233

AM 10 9 8 7 6 5 4 3 2

*To my friends and colleagues on the
San Carlos Apache reservation,
for being the bravest folks I know.*

ACKNOWLEDGMENTS

A huge shout of thanks to Noelle Pierce, Sally Kilpatrick, and Alyssa Alexander, for performing the fastest and yet most thorough beta reads possible. I don't deserve friends like you, but I'm damned glad I have you! As always, a big thank you to my agent, Kevan Lyon, and my amazing editor Tessa Woodward, as well as the entire Avon team, who work so hard on behalf of their authors. Finally, thanks to my family for understanding and tolerating the crazy.

Fling (n.): "Vigorous dance" (associated with the Scottish Highlands), from 1806. "Period of indulgence on the eve of responsibilities," first attested 1827.

FROM THE ONLINE ETYMOLOGY DICTIONARY

CHAPTER ONE

Moraig, Scotland, 1843

All the world hated a hypocrite, and William MacKenzie was no exception.

But today that trouser-clad hypocrite was his brother, James, which made it a little hard for William to hate him like he ought.

As James sauntered to a stop beneath the awning of Moraig's posting house, his laughing gaze dropped to William's bare knees and then climbed northward again. "If you're trying to make a memorable impression," he sniggered, "all that's missing is a good breeze."

"You are late." William crossed his arms and tried to look menacing. "And I thought we agreed last night we would share this indignity."

"No, *you* agreed." James shoved his hands in the pockets of his trousers and offered up a shite-eating grin. "I listened and wisely withheld a formal opinion."

William bit back a growl of frustration. For Christ's sake, he knew well enough he looked like a fool, standing in the thick heat of early August, draped in the MacKenzie plaid. And there was no doubt he would be teasing James unmercifully if the reverse were true.

But today they were *both* supposed to look like fools.

And James had a far better set of legs.

As though summoned by his brother's fateful words, a ghost of a breeze stirred the wool that clung to William's sweat-moistened skin. He clapped a hand down over his sporran, ensuring the most important parts remained hidden. "You live in Moraig, just as I do," he pointed out to his errant brother. "You owe it to the town to help me make a proper impression for the reporter from the *London Times*."

"Oh, aye, and I will. I had thought to say something properly memorable, such as 'Welcome to Moraig.'" James raised a dark, mocking brow. "And we shouldn't need to put on airs. The town has its own charm."

"Well, the tourists haven't exactly been flocking here," William retorted, gesturing to the town's nearly empty streets. Hidden in the farthest reaches of Scotland—far enough, even, that the Atlantic coast lapped at its heels— the little town of Moraig might indeed be charming, but attempts to attract London tourists had fallen somewhat short. If William had anything to say about it, that was going to change, starting today.

The only problem was he should have said it a half hour ago.

He took off his Balmoral cap and pulled his hand through hair already damp with sweat. While he was willing to tolerate looking like a fool in order to prove Moraig was the perfect holiday destination for Londoners seeking an authentic Highland experience, he still objected to having to look like one alone. "We've an opportunity to get a proper story printed in the *Times*, highlighting all Moraig has to offer." He settled the cap back on his head. "If you have an issue with the plaid, you could have at least bestirred yourself to put on a small kilt."

James burst out laughing. "And draw attention away from your bonny knees?"

As if in agreement, a series of catcalls rang out from a group of men who had crowded onto the sidewalk outside the Blue Gander, Moraig's inn and public house.

One of them held up his pint. "Lovely legs, MacKenzie!"

"Now show us your arse!"

William scowled in their direction. On another day, he might have joined them in raising a pint, but not today. Moraig's future was at stake. The town's economy was hardly prospering, and its weathered residents couldn't depend on fishing and gossip to sustain them forever. They needed a new direction, and as the Earl of Kilmartie's heir, he felt obligated to sort out a solution. He'd spent months organizing the upcoming Highland Games. It was a calculated risk that, if properly orchestrated, would ensure the betterment of every life in town. When David Cameron, the town's magistrate, had offered to invite a reporter up from London, it had seemed a brilliant opportunity to reach those very tourists they were aiming to attract.

But with the sweat now pooling in places best left unmentioned and the minutes ticking slowly by, that brilliance was beginning to tarnish.

William peered down the road that led into town, imagining he could see a cloud of dust implying the arrival of the afternoon coach. The very *late* afternoon coach. But all he saw was the delicate shimmer of heat, reflecting the nature of the devilishly hot day.

"Bugger it all," he muttered. "How late can a coach be? There's only one route from Inverness." He plucked at the damp collar of his shirt, wondering where the coachman could be. "Mr. Jeffers knew the importance of being on time today. We need to make a ripping first impression with this reporter."

James's gaze dropped once more to William's bare legs. "Oh, I don't think there's any doubt of it." He leaned against the posting house wall and crossed his arms. "If I might beg the question... Why turn it into such a circus? Why these games, instead of, say, a well-placed rumor of a beastie living in Loch Moraig? You've got the entire town in an uproar preparing for it."

William snorted. "Sunday dinners are enough to put this town in an uproar. And you know as well as I that the games are for their own good."

Though, God forbid his nolly-cocked, newly married brother lift a hand in the planning.

Or be bothered to put on a kilt, as it were.

William could allow that James was perhaps a bit distracted by his pretty wife and new baby—and understandably so. But given that his brother was raising his bairns here, shouldn't he want to ensure Moraig's future success more than anyone?

James looked up suddenly, shading his eyes with a hand. "Well, best get those knees polished to a shine. There's your coach now. Half hour late, as per usual."

With a near groan of relief, William stood at attention on the posting house steps as the mail coach roared up in a choking cloud of dust and hot wind. Scrawny chickens and stray dogs scuttled to dubious safety before the coach's barreling path, and he eyed the animals with a moment's concern, wondering if perhaps he ought to have tried to corral them into some hidden corner, safely out of sight.

But it was too late now.

A half hour off schedule. Perhaps it wasn't the tragedy he'd feared. They could skip the initial stroll down Main Street he'd planned and head straight to the inn. He could point out some of the pertinent sights later, when he showed the man the competition field that had been prepared on the east side of town.

"And dinna tell the reporter I'm the heir," William warned as an afterthought. "We want him to think of Moraig as a charming and rustic retreat from London." If the town was to have a future, it needed to be seen as a welcome escape from titles and peers and such, and he did not want this turning into a circus where he stood at the center of the ring.

As the coach groaned to a stop, James clapped William on the shoulder with mock sympathy. "Don't worry. With those bare legs, I suspect your reporter will have enough to write about without nosing about the details of your inheritance."

The coachman secured the reins and jumped down from his perch. A smile of amusement broke across Mr. Jeffers's broad features. "Wore the plaid today, did we?"

Bloody hell. Not Jeffers, too.

"You're late." William scowled. "Were there any problems fetching the chap from Inverness?" He was anxious to greet the reporter, get the man properly situated in the Blue Gander, and then go home to change into something less...*Scottish*. And, God, knew he could also use a pint or three, though preferably ones not raised at his expense.

Mr. Jeffers pushed the brim of his hat up an inch and scratched his head. "Well, see, here's the thing. I dinna exactly fetch a chap, as it were."

This time, William couldn't suppress the growl that erupted from his throat. "Mr. Jeffers, don't tell me you *left* him there!" It would be a nightmare if he had. The entire thing had been carefully orchestrated, down to a reservation for the best room the Blue Gander had to offer. The goal had been to install the reporter safely in Moraig and show him a taste of the town's charms *before* the games commenced on Saturday.

"Well, I...that is..." Mr. Jeffers's gaze swung between the brothers, and he finally shrugged. "Well, I suppose you'll see well enough for yourself."

He turned the handle and then swung the coach door open.

A gloved hand clasped Mr. Jeffers's palm, and then a high, elegant boot flashed into sight.

"What in the blazes—" William choked on his surprise as a blond head tipped into view. A body soon followed, stepping down in a froth of blue skirts. She dropped Jeffers's hand and looked around with bright interest.

"Your chap's a lass," explained a bemused Mr. Jeffers.

"A lass?" echoed William stupidly.

And not only a lass...a very pretty lass.

She smiled at the men, and it was like the sun cresting over the hills that rimmed Loch Moraig, warming all who were fortunate enough to fall in its path. William was suddenly and inexplicably consumed by the desire to recite poetry to the sound of twittering birds. That alone might have been manageable, but as her eyes met his, he was also consumed by an unfortunate jolt of lustful awareness that left every inch of him unscathed—and there were quite a few inches to cover.

"Miss Penelope Tolbertson," she said, extending her gloved hand as though she were a man. "R-reporter for the *London Times*."

He stared at her hand unsure of whether to shake it or kiss it. Her manners might be bold, but her voice was like butter, flowing over a body until it didn't know which end was up. His tongue seemed wrapped in cotton, muffling even the merest hope for a proper greeting.

The reporter was female?

And not only female...a veritable goddess, with eyes the color of a fair Highland sky.

Dimly, he felt James's elbow connect with his ribs. He knew he needed to say something. Preferably something that made the ripping first impression he'd planned.

He raised his eyes to meet hers, giving himself up to the sense of falling.

Or perhaps more aptly put, a sense of flailing.

"W-welcome to Moraig, Miss Tolbertson."

Penelope fought to keep her expression neutral.

It wasn't as though she hadn't been teased for her stammer nearly every day of her life, the merciless jeers from Brighton's summer visitors bending her but never quite breaking her.

Instead of delivering a witty retort—which experience foretold would only emphasize her infirmity—she forced herself to smile pleasantly at the man who had just delivered the insult.

Whoever he was, he looked very much like the penny-dreadful version of a Highland warrior, with his dark, windswept hair, bulging biceps, and endlessly looped plaid. Of course, the penny dreadfuls didn't make her stomach contract in quite the same nervous fashion.

And impressive or no, she had little patience for a person who thought it fun to mock a lady's stammer.

She tried to push away the stirrings of self-doubt such things always brought. Her sister, Caroline, who'd married Moraig's magistrate last year, had always sought relief from her childhood demons by swimming. But Pen had retreated from her tormentors with words—books and poetry and newspapers. Eventually she had uncovered a talent for putting her words on paper, probably because they became so tangled on her tongue. With that discovery, the anxieties about her stammer had finally begun to subside.

She did not enjoy having them rekindled today.

She turned her attentions to the more familiar gentleman standing in wait. "It is good to see you again, Mr. MacKenzie." She smiled at her sister's handsome friend and pushed a damp strand of hair from her cheek. "I must say, it is much warmer than it was d-during my last visit."

"You've visited Moraig before?" the rude Highlander interrupted.

"Yes," Pen said patiently. It seemed he was bound to either repeat questions already answered or else struggle to keep up with the conversation. She framed a gentle smile to her lips, the kind that made people nearly always underestimate her. "As I just said."

She would have liked to ignore him but suspected it would be a close to impossible task, given that he seemed nearly twice the size of most men. Her gaze scooted lower, to the thick, muscled calves peeking out from beneath the folds of fabric. She was used to her share of bare legs, growing up in Brighton as she had. But she wasn't used to legs that looked like this.

She schooled her cheeks against the flush that wanted to claim them. She would *not* blush like an adolescent schoolgirl. After all, she was an independent, modern woman, even if her tongue sometimes became a bit tied. She had boldly negotiated this position with the *London Times*—the first woman reporter they had ever hired. She had a job to do here, and she needed to do it well. It did not matter what a brawny, belted Highlander thought of her.

It mattered only what she thought of Moraig and what she chose to write about it.

In contrast to the village idiot, James MacKenzie's green eyes sparkled with mirth and intelligence. "Miss Tolbertson is David Cameron's new sister-in-law. I was fortunate enough to take dinner with them when she visited over Christmas," he explained to the befuddled giant. He cocked his head, studying her. "I must say, this is quite a surprise, Miss Tolbertson. Cameron told us to expect a reporter from London, but he didn't say it would be you. Don't you work for the *Brighton Gazette?*"

She nodded, pleased he had remembered. Then again, a female journalist was enough of a novelty she supposed it might be a difficult fact to forget. "I did. But I've just b-been awarded a position with the *Times* and moved to London." It was the first job she'd ever applied for. *Fought* for. Though her initial work with the *Brighton Gazette* had been enjoyable, she couldn't help but feel her experience didn't quite count, not when it was the newspaper her father had once founded. "This is my first formal assignment," she admitted. And even if her brother-in-law had helped procure it, she felt a driving need to make sure it went well.

"A decision we can only hope serves us both well, given our hopes for a positive outcome for Moraig." James gestured to the man standing beside him. "May I present William MacKenzie. My brother, and occasional Highland warrior when the circumstances call for it."

Pen turned back to the perspiring behemoth and studied him with greater interest. This was James MacKenzie's brother? She could imagine now seeing some resemblance there, in their shared height and dark hair, but the Highlander was far broader about the shoulders and chest, and his scowling features lacked the easy handsomeness of James's welcoming smile. Then again, Pen could allow she looked little like her sister Caroline, who was tall and brunette.

Only their penchant for impropriety identified them clearly as sisters.

She tried to smile. "P-pleased to meet you, Mr. MacKenzie."

Confused brown eyes swept her from boot to bonnet. "I dinna understand. You are saying *you* are the reporter we've been expecting from London?"

No matter his slow pattern of thought, the deep swell of his voice made her heart shift into a less-than-ladylike pattern. She couldn't countenance the reaction. Despite the impressiveness of his calves, he was none too handsome about the top. His face was as broad as his chest, lacking even a dimple to soften the stark impression of masculinity. His nose was slightly hooked, as though it had been broken once and left to set however it wished.

And there was clearly not much going on between those ears.

"Yes. *I* am the reporter," Penelope said, still smiling through her clenched teeth.

"But...I've never heard of a female reporter."

Penelope sighed. Perhaps he had belted his plaid too tightly this morning. "Perhaps not in Moraig, b-but I assure you, the world is a bit larger than this." Of course, most people outside Moraig had never heard of a female reporter either, but she didn't think it a worthy enough fact to point out. There *ought* to be more female reporters.

And she intended to prove herself an excellent one.

The coachman chose that moment to bring her valise. He held it out to William MacKenzie, but Penelope snatched it and hefted it against her chest.

"I c-can manage my own luggage," she said, perhaps a bit more forcefully than was needed. But the bag held her notebook and her pencils, the very tools of her trade, and this MacKenzie didn't seem the brightest of souls. Should her things be misplaced or mishandled, she would have a devil of a time finding replacements in a little town like Moraig.

The Highlander scowled. "It seems wrong."

A flare of irritation uncurled in Pen's stomach. "I assure you, I am a very c-capable j-journalist." She winced to hear her words begin to jam up. Her stammer always worsened when she was agitated, which was one of the reasons she tried so hard to maintain a calm, serene demeanor. But something about this man's bumbling presumptions and his bare, flexing calves made it difficult to keep her thoughts focused.

He shook his head. "No, it seems wrong, a lady carrying her own bag to the Blue Gander. What will people think?"

"Oh, I do not p-plan to stay at the Gander."

William MacKenzie's head jerked back, and his blue feathered cap fell off his head. "But…how will you report on its suitability for tourist lodging if you don't actually stay there?"

Pen narrowly avoided rolling her eyes. Did he even understand what half those words meant? He'd clearly not applied himself to the understanding of the earlier bits of the conversation. "As your b-brother said earlier, I am Mrs. Cameron's sister." She spoke slowly, so he would be sure to understand. "I had thought to s-stay in their home."

William MacKenzie stared at her, a dumbfounded expression on his broad face. Clearly she had taxed the limits of his imagination.

And he had taxed the limits of her tolerance.

She turned to James MacKenzie, knowing that there, at least, there was a spark of intelligence she could rely on. "Mr. MacKenzie, might I b-beg upon your assistance? I had not written ahead of the timing of my visit. I had hoped to surprise Caroline, you see."

The younger MacKenzie chuckled. "I'd be happy take you to Cameron's house." He gestured her forward but wisely made no move to relieve her of her bag. "And if a wee bit of surprise was your hope for the day, I'd say well done." A crooked grin split his face. "I don't believe I've ever seen my brother rendered speechless before."

CHAPTER TWO

"**S**he thinks I'm an idiot." William stared moodily down at his drink as the familiar scents and sounds of the Blue Gander's dinnertime crowd swam around him.

Normally, he quite enjoyed the buzz of the inn's little public room. But tonight, he felt the clink of every dish like a bolt to the brain, reminding him that he was, in fact, the very blooming idiot Miss Tolbertson no doubt suspected him to be.

Welcome to Moraig, he had said to her. Such a scintillating welcome.

And then he had stammered it, no less.

He groaned and knocked his head against the scarred and pitted surface of the table, though he was probably rubbing his face in week-old spilled ale. Miss Tolbertson's stammer hadn't bothered him in the least. But he was quite sure his own tongue-tied performance would be long remembered in her mind.

"A smart lass then, is she?" McRory took a noisy gulp of ale and slammed his cup down on the table. "Pretty too, from what Jeffers said."

William opened a wary eye from his position on the table and glared up at the town butcher. "Too pretty for the likes of you," he snarled feebly. Though he was long used to Moraig's rumor mill, his drinking companion's words made him want to smash something, and the nearest satisfying target was McRory's thick skull.

He straightened. And what business did the very married Mr. Jeffers have bandying news of Miss Tolbertson's attractiveness about town?

Although, to be fair, attractive unmarried females were not exactly bursting from Moraig's seams, and gossip was the town's stock-in-trade. Why in the deuces was he feeling so protective of her? The woman could obviously take care of herself. She hadn't even brought a maid with her and had still managed to look as fresh as a flower upon emerging from the depths of the coach. An image of her clear blue eyes, glaring at him above the top of her bag, was practically seared into his brain.

Still, McRory *did* have a bit of a reputation for inviting unsuspecting women to a sit-down in his lap, especially when he was into his cups.

And they were both well into the fourth of those cups this evening.

But regardless of McRory's reputation, it wasn't as though Miss Tolbertson needed his protection tonight. She clearly had no intention of setting foot anywhere close to the Blue Gander. Why, she'd practically sprinted to Cameron's house, ruining William's grand plans to showcase the town's inn as the focal point of Moraig's appeal to London tourists. He thought morosely about the room he'd personally paid to refurbish above stairs, expressly for the purpose of impressing a London reporter.

Of course, he hadn't known the reporter was a *lass* at the time, had he?

Nothing about the day's events had followed his carefully arranged plans, and that left him floundering in more than the bottom of a glass.

Dimly, he became aware that McRory wasn't answering him. In fact, the tenor of the entire crowd had shifted. Hushed, even. A nearly impossible accomplishment for an establishment as infamously rowdy as the Gander. Why, his own brother had once knocked out McRory's teeth, there on the main floor, and then busted out the row of front windows to boot.

The pub hadn't been quiet that night, to hear the rumors. Nor any night since.

William shifted in his seat and fixed his bleary gaze on the door, only to promptly catch his breath. Christ, she *was* seared into his brain. Because there she was, his thoughts most happily playing this cruel trick on him. As before, he felt strangely hobbled by the impact of those blue eyes, the way her upper lip curved prettily. *Invitingly.*

If this was an ale-fueled dream, it was a gashing good one.

But then the blond-haired apparition moved.

Straight into the middle of the Blue Gander's public room.

Chairs everywhere scraped the floor as man after man gained his feet. William stayed hunkered down in his seat, though he would have happily crawled beneath the sticky floor boards if given half a chance. He was rewarded for his ill manners by staying somewhere beneath her notice. She smiled a pleasant greeting at all and sundry and then took a seat at an empty table, looking around her with undisguised interest. She took off her bonnet and gloves and then placed her reticule on the table and began to rummage through it.

That was apparently all the invitation required.

McRory lunged in her direction, and William had to reach out a hand and haul the butcher back by the tail of his bloodstained apron strings. "Sit your arse back down," he warned.

"Why?" McRory scowled down at him. "She dinna say she thinks *I'm* an idiot."

"Yet," William retorted. "The night is young." He sniffed, taking in a whiff of sour male and the faint hint of offal. "You're too ripe by half for a lady's company tonight, and I'll not have you mauling the reporter who's come to save the town from economic disaster. You'll have her writing that every London tourist is invited to sit on the butcher's lap."

McRory slowly lowered his bulk back into his chair. "If they are pretty as that one," he said, leering, "they're welcome to sit wherever they want."

William's fists tightened. Oh, for God's sake.

That was all Moraig needed, word of McRory's lap to reach London.

He slouched down in his seat, though he kept his surreptitious attention on Miss Tolbertson. He hoped she knew what she was about, gallivanting around town without an escort. Presumably a female reporter was hardier than the usual sort of woman, and Moraig was a safer town than most. But God knew her table wouldn't stay empty long, not in a place like this. He felt the slow burn of respect at the thought of her bravery.

Bloody hell, the woman walked about as though she were a man.

But she didn't look like a man. She looked like an angel, and William was halfway to heaven just watching her give her order to the serving girl.

And praise the saints, she ordered whisky. Not one, but *three* glasses of the stuff, different varieties. From the corner of his eye, he watched in horror and fascination as she delicately sniffed one, then the other, and then—God above—lifted one of the glasses to her lips and took an ambitious swallow.

She immediately began to choke, eyes squeezed shut, lungs straining for air.

William was on his feet and halfway across the floor, ignoring McRory's shout of protest, when she gathered herself for a proper breath. Unfortunately, his chivalry had the misfortune of placing him squarely in her line of sight as her eyes snapped open.

Her shocked gaze met his, five seconds of time that felt like a match set to paper. Her fair brow furrowed, and he felt again that jolt of lust—fueled, this time, by four of the best draughts of ale the Blue Gander had to offer.

And then she bent her head.

It was only then that William realized she held in her hand a leather-bound notebook and was scribbling furiously in it with a pencil.

Well. She might stay alone at her table if she acted like *that*. Academically accomplished females were even rarer in Moraig than attractive ones, and the Gander's usual sort of patron had no idea what to do with one besides stare at them. She would probably stay safe enough if she kept that pencil clasped in her pretty hand.

Despite the lack of an obvious need for his assistance, William forced his feet to continue their forward trajectory. After all, she had seen him. No point hiding now. At least he was wearing trousers this time, his great hairy knees properly covered and his more frightening parts safe from the odd breeze. She was prudently covered as well. In fact, she looked a proper lady, no excess bit of skin visible anywhere on her person. But William was possessed of a solid imagination, and his mouth was already watering over the possibilities that lay beneath.

He wanted to say something witty. Something better than a stammered greeting. But despite the fact he counted a Cambridge education among his list of accomplishments, his tongue was apparently still as tied tonight as it had been this afternoon.

He paused in front of her table and grunted like a peasant.

Blue eyes raised to his. "Was there s-something you wanted, MacKenzie?" she choked out, still suffering the residual effects of her brush with the whisky.

Bloody hell, she even addressed him like a man. And his brain was apparently not as tied as his tongue, because inside his skull, a refrain echoed: *I want you.*

For once, he was glad of his limited abilities for actual speech while in her presence.

"Er...I came to ask if you knew what you were doing."

She wiped her watering eyes on the edge of a napkin. "Research, of course."

Christ, he really *was* an idiot. She was a reporter. Reporters researched things. And if there was one thing Moraig could boast to London tourists, it was twelve varieties of a good Highland whisky.

"Ah, I remember my first brush with a Highland malt. Much the same reaction as yours. 'Tis the sort of taste one acquires with time and practice." He slid into the wooden bench across the table from her and pointed to the glass that held the darkest liquid. "Someone should warn you that this one is rather potent. And the previous lass who did this sort of research at the Blue Gander wound up married."

Blue eyes widened. "To *you?*"

He chuckled, the words coming easier now. "No. To my brother, James. Not that the lady minded in the end, you ken."

"That sounds intriguing." She leaned forward across the table. "T-tell me more."

William grinned. It was a relief to know his tongue could still work with a little effort. "It was quite the scandal at the time. Now they've a bonny wee babe to bounce on their knee."

Her blond head bent down, and she scribbled something in her notebook.

William felt a frisson of foreboding. "I don't believe... that is... Their courtship is not something you should write about."

"Oh?" she asked, still writing furiously. "I thought I was invited here to expressly write about Moraig's charms." She looked up at him, though her hand kept flying across the page. "And it's very a charming story. T-tell me, how does one usually get married in Moraig?"

William hesitated, distracted as hell by the sight of her talking and writing at the same time. "The blacksmith most often does the honors. And...ah...Reverend Ramsey, if the couple wants a church wedding."

"And your brother's wedding," she pressed. Her nonoccupied hand slid the darkest glass of whisky toward him, as though inviting him to share. "What sort of ceremony d-did they have? You mentioned the lady was inebriated?"

William's chest squeezed tight, and he sought a moment's respite by tossing the proffered glass back. His brain was definitely muddled, and not only by the ale. He could handle four pints. What he was beginning to doubt he could handle was Miss Tolbertson.

Now would be a good time for his tongue to retie itself. The story wasn't a secret, per se. In fact, the circumstances of his brother's impromptu wedding came closer to legend around these parts. But he felt rather protective of Georgette, his new sister-in-law, and truly, the events of that night had not been her fault at all.

Through his panicked musings, the pencil scratched merrily on. William stared at it, half fascinated, half appalled. Christ, but Miss Tolbertson was tenacious. He was beginning to have an inkling she was probably an excellent reporter.

And that meant he needed to be a bit more careful around her.

William reached out a hand and stilled the pencil's furious progress. "Has anyone ever told you about the mysterious creatures that inhabit Loch Moraig?" he asked, thinking as quickly as his addled brain would permit.

"Are you referring to water d-dragons?" A pale, perfect brow arched high. "Several bodies of water in this region boast such creatures. That hardly makes Moraig special."

William blinked, already mortified he had said such a thing. *Out loud.* Damn his brother for putting such a ridiculous idea in his head. He might have had a few pints and a glass of whisky, but he was also an educated man, hardly believing in such things, even if some of the more superstitious town residents still spoke of wraiths and other creatures that would drag a man to his death.

And Moraig *was* special. He would prove it to her yet.

But he needed tourists to want to come here for a restorative holiday, not fear for their lives if they dipped a toe in the loch's waters. "No, I refer to *crodh mara*, of course."

She laid down her pencil. "Crodh mara?"

"Aye." He nodded. "Water cattle."

"Really." Her lips pursed into a heart-stopping smile. "C-cattle seem so much less..."

"Fearsome?" William leaned back, feeling rather proud of himself for thinking of it.

She shook her head and laughed. "Charming."

Pen watched as surprise and good humor flitted across MacKenzie's broad face.

Though this afternoon he'd seemed a rather empty vessel, tonight he wore his every thought openly. Was this really the same gruff man who'd greeted her so rudely outside the posting house? He seemed more relaxed. Or perhaps that was just an effect of a mild intoxication. He really was rather sweet, trying so hard to convince her of Moraig's appeal.

But he needn't bother. The town *was* charming.

Far more charming than London, which had done little to impress her with anything beyond its sheer size and head-spinning bustle. Though she'd only just moved to the city, she was already questioning how she might live there. As a result of her impoverished Brighton upbringing, she'd come to expect a certain freedom of movement beyond that which most ladies enjoyed. But she certainly couldn't move about London without an escort, or else she risked being accosted on the street. And after experiencing the summer stink of the Thames firsthand, she could see why the city's residents fled to more pastoral places when the temperatures soared.

Though she was still none too impressed with the man's intelligence—blathering on as he was about mythical creatures—she was marginally impressed that MacKenzie had at least shown enough sense to deflect her questions about his brother's marriage.

She was a reporter. It was her lot in life to ask probing questions.

But it was equally clear that *his* lot in life was to protect his family and his town, and that was something she could not help but respect.

Still, she couldn't resist teasing him a bit now. "If you would like me to report on these water cattle, then by all means, do go on." She picked up her pencil again. "Are they very large creatures?" She tapped the pencil against her lips.

"Perhaps they b-bellow a warning to unsuspecting boats, warning them of the water dragons?"

His lips twitched. He leaned forward, and she was surprised to find herself dragged into the warm depths of his eyes. "Crodh mara are not to be trifled with, lass." He lifted his hands, pantomiming horns. "They've gored all the water dragons, you see. But that's a good thing, because now it's quite safe for the tourists to walk about *our* loch."

She couldn't help it. She laughed out loud.

He chuckled as well, and with that shared intimacy, warmth spread through her that had nothing to do with the whisky she'd gulped. Tonight, there was something about his easy grin that threatened to lay waste to the poor initial impression he'd made. She was tempted to believe that perhaps he'd not meant to mock her this afternoon.

Moreover, both James MacKenzie and David Cameron had insisted that William MacKenzie was the man to speak to if she had any questions related to the upcoming Highland Games, so she knew she needed to further this acquaintance.

And heaven help her, the way he'd said "crodh mara," with a caress of brogue, made her stomach tilt in new and dangerous directions. Then, of course, there was the matter of his well-made legs to contend with—the memory of which made the blush she had fought off so valiantly this afternoon return in full measure.

She was disturbed enough to take another sip of one of the remaining glasses of whisky—a smaller taste, this time. She tasted peat and smoke and an underlying hint of salt. It went down far more smoothly than her first swallow. She blinked in astonishment.

Was William MacKenzie much the same as the whisky?

Something to choke down at the first but then savor later?

She took another sip and then set down her glass, curiously studying his profile as he called the serving girl to their table. Though he wasn't the swiftest of men—or even the most handsome man in the room—there was something about him that made her want to lean across the table and brush her lips against that wide, laughing mouth.

The serving girl strolled up to their table, with eyes only for the gentleman. "Ready for another pint, then?" She was a buxom, brunette thing, and she cocked her hip, clearly willing to serve up whatever MacKenzie wished. "Or have your thoughts finally turned to something more pleasurable? You know you need only ask."

Pen's cheeks heated. Despite her thirst for adventure, she'd led a somewhat sheltered life, living in genteel poverty with her mother and sister in Brighton. Even with this recent move to London, she'd made sure to find lodging in a respectable establishment, and had kept to well-lit paths. She'd never heard such a blatant offer made to a gentleman before.

Then again, she'd never set foot in a tavern before, either.

It was a night of several firsts, and she was feeling a bit lightheaded as a result.

MacKenzie tossed a coin out on the table. "No, Sally, none of that now. We want to be on our best behavior for the reporter who's come to make Moraig famous. I only want to pay for Miss Tolbertson's attempt to research our whisky, as we're leaving now."

A bit of Pen's pleasure faded, though she was glad to hear he didn't intend to leave with the serving girl. She didn't want to be disappointed in this man, now that she had finally sorted out there was a bit more to him than she had first presumed.

But was he one of *those* gentlemen, who believed a lady must be ensconced at home or escorted everywhere? She encountered far too many of the sort in the course of her daily work. And as she had no reputation she planned to preserve—having already firmly committed herself to spinsterhood and the shocking impropriety of having a profession—she was ill inclined to bow to such whims now.

As the servant left, the coin safely tucked between her generous breasts, Pen leaned in. "Perhaps I am not yet ready to g-go, MacKenzie," she warned.

"'Tis your choice, of course." He turned back to face her. "But I can see you don't believe me, lass." His voice deepened. "So I've a mind to show you the crodh mara by moonlight. 'Tis said to be when their magic is strongest."

The pleasure rushed back in. "Oh," she whispered.

"You're a courageous thing, I'll allow. Not many women would try their hand at a malt. But I suppose it stands to be seen whether you're brave enough to risk a stroll down by Loch Moraig."

Something in his voice, and in his eyes as well, told her he'd be willing to show her more than water cattle, if only she were brave enough to want that, too. Pen knew that to most people, she appeared the sort of woman who would happily spend her days lost in a book. But he wasn't looking at her the way most gentlemen did, as though they saw only a twenty-six-year-old spinster with a stammer. No, he was looking at her as though he understood her motivations, and that was a novelty she wanted to explore.

It surprised her that MacKenzie seemed to see more in her than most. She enjoyed nothing so much as the challenge of trying new things, probably because so much of her life in Brighton had been lived in the opposite fashion. She had taken the job in London because her fledgling success with Brighton's small newspaper had made her want more. She'd come here alone tonight because she'd wanted the freedom to view the town in its natural state, rather than through the eyes of a tightly chaperoned female.

She had every confidence that if she found the right gentleman, she would want to try other things as well, things she heretofore had only read about in books.

And heaven help her, William MacKenzie made her feel…curious.

In Brighton, this sort of invitation could mean only one thing. Not that she had ever received such an invitation herself, mind you, but even a spinster deserved a first real kiss. So she rose, shoving her notebook and pencil in her reticule and gathering up her bonnet and gloves.

"Lead the way, MacKenzie."

He chuckled, making her stomach somersault once more as he gestured toward the door. "Ach, lass, don't you think you might call me 'William'? After all, a man who's paid for your drinks might have earned the privilege, aye?"

CHAPTER THREE

In Brighton, the night skies of her childhood had carried the reflection of the moon off the water and the faint echoes of a thousand candles and oil lamps. During her brief time in London, the night had blazed nearly as bright as day, the sky obscured by smoke and smog and the sidewalks shimmering in gaslight shadows.

But in Scotland, it seemed the night sky turned itself over to the stars.

It was still warm, but with the night air came a mixture of scents she had missed when she first arrived. Sharp pine and mellow heather. The coastal tang of the breeze coming from the west. And beneath it all, growing stronger now as Pen picked her way along the dark path, the dusky scent of water and bogs and lurking animal life.

"Almost there," MacKenzie murmured over his shoulder. "Quietly now. They startle easy."

She smiled into the darkness, given that the idea of mythical creatures startling anyone was a bit of a lark. She had come down here for a reason, and she hoped the experience of her first real kiss—with a gentleman not obligated as a result of a parlor game—was a duly memorable one.

Pen tilted her face up, nearly as mesmerized by the spangled sky as the whisky-rich sound of MacKenzie's voice. How far had they come? A half mile, perhaps, but it felt as though they had gone straight down the side of a cliff, picking their way over rocks and roots alike. She'd been forced to grab his hand on more than one occasion. It had been necessary, that last grab, when her fingers had lingered over his. She refused to entertain the idea that perhaps she had reached for his hand for less than required reasons.

She felt no hesitation, only a breathless anticipation that made everything seem more acute. Even when her feet tripped over unseen objects, she was not afraid. Her Highlander might be a bit dim, but he was also big and powerful, and she had no doubts at all he would protect her.

They emerged from the steep path and stepped out into a clearing, and that was when she heard a low, unearthly moan that sent her heart pounding in a sudden gust of fear.

He held up a hand, halting their progress.

"MacKenzie?" she whispered. "What was that?"

His only answer was a sharp, high-pitched whistle.

The bellow came again, followed by a distant splashing. The moon shone down on the surface of the loch like a bonfire, and in its light she caught a ghastly shadow.

Her hand came up to catch her gasp of terror. She hadn't believed him, back at the tavern. She'd thought this little more than folktale, the sort of yarn spun to convince young ladies to sneak out for a moonlit kiss. Not that she had needed much convincing.

But as something lumbered ashore in the darkness, she realized she was more than halfway to believing him now.

She leaped forward like a startled rabbit, plastering herself against MacKenzie's solid back and all but mounting him in a tangle of skirts. "What *is* that?" she hissed.

He chuckled, and she could feel the movement of his big body through every inch of her front, pressed against him as she was. "Crodh mara," he whispered. "As I told you."

"But…they are mythical c-creatures," she protested, praying it was true.

But *something* was out there.

And that something was making its way toward them.

He put a steadying hand on her waist. "Easy, lass. They can smell fear."

And oh, merciful heavens, she could smell *them*, a musty, waterlogged scent that made her want to wrinkle her nose. She peered around his shoulder in a panic. Along the shoreline, something else moved.

Something big and terrifying and coming her way.

They are not real, she told herself fiercely. *He only brought you down here for a kiss.*

But the moan came again, closer now, and deep and soul shaking.

"I want to go b-back, please." She buried her face in the expanse of his back, the linen of his shirt scraping against her goose-pebbled skin. "Take me back."

"Aye. Soon. But if you don't greet them, they'll only follow you up the hill." He pulled her around to his side. His fingers curled where they made contact with her waist, and she could feel his calm strength through the thin fabric. "Better, I think, to face them, now that you've come this far."

She willed herself to trust in the steadying hand that hovered near her hip.

She drew a shuddering breath and looked up.

Oh, God. They looked like nothing she had ever seen before, in books or otherwise. Certainly, nothing like this shaggy, waterlogged creature had ever washed up on the shores of Brighton. In the moonlight, it seemed the size of a London omnibus, with horns longer than a man's leg.

"Some say the crodh mara are fairies," MacKenzie said, his voice deep and strangely hypnotic, though whether it was fashioned to render her or the creatures frozen, she couldn't be sure. "But I've always had a more practical view of the beasts."

One of the dark, lumbering creatures came closer. MacKenzie held out his hand, as though he held heaven and earth in it. The thing butted its huge head against the outstretched palm, knocking them both off balance. Pen squeaked in fear and surprise.

"And of course," he chuckled, "they like a wee bit of sugar."

He loosened his hold on her, one hand digging in his trouser pocket, and then, as she watched in mute fear and wonder, he stretched his hand out again, a biscuit in his palm.

The creature took it with a delicate swipe of its tongue.

"They're…real?" Pen whispered, growing braver now. Any creature who liked biscuits was one she could perhaps comprehend. She looked up at MacKenzie, her eyes searching his. "I d-don't understand."

"Every legend is anchored in fact, aye?" He handed her another biscuit, dug from the depths of his pocket. "These are a breed of cattle unique to the Highlands. *Kyloe*, we call them. These are my personal breeding stock." He rubbed an affectionate hand on the creature's nose.

Pen stared at him, incredulous. "You brought me here to show me your c-cattle?"

"My *water* cattle." In the moonlight, she could see the flash of his teeth. "They are great hairy beasts, and so they spend a good deal of time in the water on hot summer days, only coming out at night."

Her heart was still pounding like a hammer in her chest, but more in wonder now than fear. Her natural curiosity began to overcome her surprise. "Can I touch them?" she asked. At his nod, Pen slowly reached out her palm. She'd seen cattle before, of course. They littered the Sussex countryside and were driven into Brighton on market days. But those cattle had looked nothing like this shaggy, dripping beast.

She felt the roughened swipe of its tongue. The warm breath and slick surface of its nose.

And then her hand was licked clean, and she was laughing in delight.

More inquisitive bodies crowded in. It seemed MacKenzie had brought biscuits enough for them all. Seemed, as well, as though he did this with some regularity. He called them by name, soft Gaelic words she didn't understand but that made her heart thump louder and that obviously meant something to the eager creatures.

Oighrig. Cadha. Beathas. Caileach.

She took care to keep her feet out of reach of their milling, sharp hooves, watching more than participating. And then finally, his pockets were emptied.

"I think we are safe enough to go now." He wiped his hands on his trousers as the cattle began to lumber away. "Once they've had their treat, they are usually content to let me leave." He gestured to the steep hillside. "The path is just there."

Pen's cheeks warmed. "Must we g-go quite yet?"

He smiled down at her, shadowed by moonlight. "Waiting for a water dragon, then?" She felt the air stir as he stepped nearer, and his low, earthy chuckle brushed tantalizingly against her ears. "Or perhaps a *brollachan*?"

Her knees quivered at the sound of the unfamiliar word. "What is a brollachan?"

"A shapeless creature of the night."

Pen's gaze swept down his moon-soaked frame, and a shiver snaked its way up her spine. She was a journalist. A manipulator of words. And "shapeless" was not a word she would ever reach for to describe William MacKenzie.

In his plaid, he had been fiercely magnificent.

In moonlight, he was devastating.

"I j-just want to enjoy the moment," she whispered. "The n-night is lovely, after all." She flushed to hear her stammer was worsening, but there was no denying she felt anything but calm and serene. She had come down here for a reason, and despite the beauty of the surprise he'd offered her, that reason had not yet been realized. "Did you really just bring me here to see your c-cattle?" she blurted out.

Dark eyes glittered down at her, nearly handsome in their unswerving focus. "I thought you might like to write about them. They are part of what make the Highlands special." He paused. "Why? What else did you hope to see, Miss Tolbertson? I would be happy to show you anything you wish during your time here."

"I p-prefer to explore on my own." It was said before Pen had time to think. Though it was the truth, she regretted her haste. She could think of worse ways to spend her days in Moraig than strolling the picturesque streets on this man's very muscular arm.

"Aye. I've noticed," he said with a tight smile. "But you might consider using a guide. There is a good deal of history in the town, and we want you to have a favorable impression, after all."

Pen swallowed. In truth, her impression was improving with every passing second, and not only of Moraig. She thought of how this man's body had felt pressed against hers, when she had thrown herself against him. Safe and disturbing, all at once. But he seemed to have no intention of kissing her. And why would he? The buxom serving girl in the Gander had offered him far more than a kiss, and *she* didn't have a stammer.

Worse, he had brought her here, shown her these mysterious, moon-soaked creatures, only because he imagined she would want to write about it. And she should.

She *would*.

But for Pen, it was a night of firsts, and she couldn't see ending it without reaching for the experience she most desired. And after all, he'd just offered to show her anything she wished.

She stepped forward, going up on her toes, and fisted her hands in his shirt. Her lips bumped against his. And then she threw herself into her very first kiss.

He stilled, as though wrapping his head around what she was offering.

Dim as a rock, she thought, closing her eyes. How could he not see what she wanted?

But then his arms came up around her, and that was when her thoughts became muddled. Because the kiss she had sought—the kiss she had taken, really—shifted into something no longer under her control. She was pulled against his chest with a solid, welcome thump, and then his mouth moved over hers, murmuring in a soft brogue that made no sense but turned her into little more than a quiver.

And his kiss…He might be a bit dull about the edges, but in this area he was proving well educated. It was clear the man knew how to kiss a woman properly. It was impossible to do it justice with mere words. She turned herself over to the sheer feel of it. Every sense she possessed—and some she hadn't realized she had—felt plundered by the contact of his mouth on hers. Stripped bare.

Reformed in the shape of this moment.

He tasted of Scotland: dark and smoky, heat and salt. The scrape of his whiskered jaw and the solid strength in his body made her hum with an unspoken awareness.

She kissed him blindly, her arms stretching up around his neck, body arching against his in an invitation she didn't even understand. And oh, dear heavens, how he kissed her back. His hands came up, tilting her face up to meet his mouth more fully. His tongue swept against hers, sure and swift and tasting of whisky, and she whimpered in welcome, unable to articulate how perfect it felt.

But the sound seemed to mean something different to him, and he broke away, panting.

"Christ above, lass." His hands loosened, falling away. "I dinna mean to take such advantage of you." His voice seemed to crack at the edges. "I need you, you see."

Her breath caught in her throat. "You…need me?"

"Aye." He pulled a hand across his mouth, as though the taste of her still lingered there. "That is, Moraig needs you. I would offer you an apology." He shook his head. "I'll not have you thinking all Highlanders behave this way."

Pen didn't know whether to laugh or moan in embarrassment. Because merciful heavens, if all Highlanders kissed this way, she was *never* going back to London.

If he chose to take the blame for the impropriety, she supposed she should be grateful, but part of her wanted only to press her lips against his again and see where this might lead.

"Think nothing of it, MacKenzie," she forced herself to say. "C-consider it a bit of research. Nothing more."

His brow tipped down. "Research?"

She nodded, already taking a step toward the path that would carry her floating feet back to the Blue Gander. "Like the whisky."

She left him then, scurrying up the steep hillside. Left him looking as big and confused as he had this afternoon at the posting house, but this time she couldn't help but smile at the thought. Her head was buzzing with all the glorious contradictions inherent in a kiss of this sort.

No, they should not have done it.

Yes, she wanted to do it again, and despite his gallantry, she suspected he did, too.

And *maybe*…just maybe, there was more to research than whisky on this trip.

Chapter Four

"She thinks I'm an idiot." William gave vent to the past two days of frustration, pounding a nail into the wood with a ferocity that would have no doubt served his ancestors well in battle.

"Probably, given that I do as well." James smirked, handling his own hammer with easy precision, despite the fact they were balanced some twenty feet off the ground. "In fact, half the town thinks you're an idiot for organizing the games in the heat of late summer. The other clans favor autumn for their events for a reason."

"The timing was part of the plan," William muttered. "We dinna want to compete with the others. And your bonny wife assured me that Londoners are eager to flee the city this time of the year, when the Season is over and the stink off the river becomes too great. We want them to come to Moraig." He breathed in, fresh air and newly cut lumber filling his lungs. "They'll not have to worry about a stink here."

"They will if they meet McRory," James pointed out, laughing. He wiped a hand across his brow and then shimmied higher on the scaffolding they were helping to erect, the sun glinting off his sweating shoulders. "But you didn't let me finish. Half the town is grumbling, true enough. The other half of the town thinks you are a bloody hero and are practicing for the games as we speak."

William scowled down at a grassy field below, where market days were usually held. It was already set up for the coming competition, with areas roped off for the various events. McRory was taking shameless advantage of the early preparations, and he'd been tossing a caber about for the better part of an hour, grunts and groans and the occasional feral cry of triumph floating upward on the breeze. William couldn't help but feel the butcher's efforts might be better directed toward something useful. Such as making sure there was enough beef for the arrival of their always-ravenous clansmen.

Or picking up a bloody hammer and nail.

"I'm no hero," he scoffed. "I'm only concerned for the town's future, given that I enjoy living here." He set another nail to the board he was working. "But 'tis neither here nor there. Miss Tolbertson thinks I'm an idiot because I showed her my cattle, not because of the games."

"Your cattle?" His brother's quick grin peered down at him, haloed by the sun. "Is *that* what you are calling it?"

William's ears burned. "I'll thank you to remember she's a lady." *A lady who kisses like a siren.* Even now, the thought of how close he had come to mauling her made his stomach clench. Why, oh why couldn't he have just stayed tongue-tied and clod faced around her?

Things had been so much simpler—and safer—then.

"Aye. I know she's a lady." His brother shrugged. "But I also know better than most that ladies are capable of some surprising things, especially when their inhibitions are lowered." He placed another nail and hammered it home. "All of the Gander saw her order three whiskies and then watched you leave together. You know how gossip runs in this town."

William groaned. Bloody hell, he hadn't thought of that. Too much ale in his belly, apparently, and not enough sense in his head. "She dinna have more than a sip." He glared at his brother. "I'll not have you thinking it was her idea. And nothing unforgivable happened."

Thanks only to that small sound she had made there in her throat that told him just how inexperienced she was—and just how dangerous a game they played.

"Unforgivable." James studied the head of his hammer, as though it held the secret to life. "There's an interesting word choice. Not one that normally comes to mind where cattle are concerned. Women, on the other hand—"

"Has anyone ever told you you're a sodding fool?" William snarled.

"On occasion." James grinned. "Besides, your Miss Tolbertson told Caroline, who told Georgette, who told *me*, that she quite enjoyed meeting your cattle. So don't take offense. The lady herself spoke of it."

William winced, though he was glad to hear that perhaps it hadn't been as big a blunder as he had feared. He still didn't know what he had been thinking.

Well, hell. Yes, he did. He *hadn't* been thinking. And that had the potential to become a significant problem around Miss Tolbertson. His thoughts went completely to shite around her, and then his tongue just naturally seemed to follow suit.

"Did she say anything else?" he asked hopefully. Pathetically.

James guffawed. "Ask her yourself." He pointed down at the street with his hammer. "Here she comes now."

William whipped around and nearly lost his balance. He tottered a moment on the brink of a spill, hands flailing, nails spilling down like deadly rain.

But what a way to go, watching Miss Tolbertson sashay down Main Street.

He regained his balance with an oath and a prayer and then stared in stupefied wonder as she stopped and scribbled something down in that omnipresent notebook. He hoped it was something positive—the woman seemed determined to sniff out potentially damaging things about the town. He swallowed at the sight of her blond hair, several strands of which had come down from their moorings and were whipping about the edges of her bonnet in the light breeze. He had touched that hair two nights ago. Held it in his fingers as he'd kissed her.

Nothing unforgivable happened, he reminded himself.

Other than that he'd proven himself a grand idiot, a fact that was probably now recorded in perpetuity somewhere in that notebook.

She was thoroughly and unapologetically alone, and he was coming to understand this was her preferred method of research. He'd never met a woman—at least, a woman as refined as Miss Tolbertson—who was so comfortable with the impropriety. He hadn't planned for this. For *her*. She'd laid a torch to his carefully made plans since the moment she stepped down from the coach, and he was at a loss to know what to do next with her.

Escort her around town, the offer of which she had already eschewed?

Or continue to avoid her as he had for the past two days, which was probably safer for them both?

"We offered her the loan of Elsie, Georgette's maid, who knows nearly everyone in town and a bit of colorful history besides," James said from somewhere above him. "But Miss Tolbertson said she would rather go without. Something about wanting to form her opinions through the eyes of a tourist, not the eyes of an escort."

"She would. She prefers to work alone," William murmured, so absorbed in the sight of her it took him a moment to realize his brother was looking down at him with hooded speculation, and that perhaps he had revealed more than he should.

"Why are you staring?" William asked gruffly, swinging his hammer again.

"I've never seen you so befuddled with a woman."

"I am not befuddled."

And he wasn't. Befuddled implied confusion, and even when trying to look down at his work, William was possessed with an almost clairvoyant focus, more aware of her than anything else on the street. As he tried to return to his work, his gaze pulled hard to the right as she waved at McRory, her notebook in one hand. His hammer came down on his thumb, splitting his nail.

"Oh, bloody hell!"

"Aye." James nodded sagely. "*Befuddled*."

William tried not to notice as Miss Tolbertson spent a full ten minutes speaking with the butcher. Or that McRory eagerly abandoned his practice to answer her questions, going even so far as to strike a manly pose, flexing muscles here and yon. Instead, William vented his frustration in hard work, knowing the music stage he and James were building was every bit as important to the success of the upcoming games as a hundred tossed capers.

And whom Miss Tolbertson chose to research next was none of his business.

Penelope cocked half an ear toward her subject, but all the while her mind was awash with the image of William MacKenzie, balanced like an ape on the bit of scaffolding being erected in the center of town.

Not that she had ever seen apes in anything beyond a book of exotic creatures, mind you. But one could learn a lot from books.

It was finding a way to acquire proper true-life experiences that was the struggle.

From the moment she'd seen him, bare chested and gleaming with the sweat of hard, honest work, she'd been nearly unable to take her eyes from him. Oh, she knew it wasn't a sight a proper lady should admit enjoying. The men on Brighton's beaches wore swimming garments that covered such parts. But coupled with the glimpse of his bare legs she'd been given in front of the posting house, she'd arguably seen more of this man's body than she'd seen of any other, except, perhaps, her own.

Though she turned her back on the tempting scene in an attempt to at least *appear* interested in what Mr. McRory was saying, her cheeks burned in bright awareness. She was beginning to realize that these Highlanders were an attractive—if sometimes poorly clad—lot. James MacKenzie and her brother-in-law were excellent examples of the species. Even Mr. McRory exuded a certain manly charm, tossing that great log about as though it weighed no more than goose down. The female tourists from London would find much to look at during their visits to Moraig, of that Pen had no doubt.

And William MacKenzie was proving most compelling of the lot.

"I understand you are a local b-businessman, Mr. McRory," she murmured distractedly. For her first assignment with the *Times*, her story needed to be something more spectacular than the scenery—be it moonlit lochs or bare, brawny chests. She wanted to dig deeper into the lives of the town residents, uncovering their hopes and dreams and fears. "Tell me, d-do you think the fortunes of Moraig's residents will really be improved by the Highland Games?"

"Fortunes?" The butcher slapped a meaty thigh and then grinned, showing a gap where his two front teeth ought to have gone. "William MacKenzie's not out to make us a fortune, you ken, only to save us. The harvest failed last year, and the herring runs are doing poorly. The businesses in town are only just scraping by. I dinna know what we'd do without his help."

Penelope's interest sharpened, the sounds of the hammers fading into the background. "What does Mr. MacKenzie have to d-do with the games?" she pressed. James and David had both implied MacKenzie might be able to answer any questions she had, but neither had suggested he was a primary party in the event.

And it was easier to take her mind off the shirtless man working behind her when he was the topic of the current conversation.

"Ach, lass, dinna tell me you haven't heard." McRory leaned in, waving his hirsute arms. "He's only organized the entire thing, down to the last piper. He's the only one in town smart enough to put some effort behind making something more of Moraig." He grinned. "But I'm still going to trounce him in the caber toss, come Saturday."

Pen's pencil stilled, trying to reconcile the butcher's view of the man with the bumbling giant who'd greeted her at the posting house and who'd gone on to kiss her by moonlight.

Of course, he hadn't been bumbling *then*.

"You b-believe MacKenzie is intelligent?" she asked, curious. She was no longer sure what she believed herself. Her first impression had been lackluster, but she could admit that during the course of their moonlit conversation, her brawny Highlander had actually been rather articulate, even though he'd clearly had a bit to drink. Moreover, organizing an event like the Highland Games required a good deal of planning, and no small amount of creativity.

Such things did not fit with the image of a blundering fool.

"Oh, aye. Spent four years studying at university. Top of his class at Cambridge, to hear the rumors. Summa someaught." McRory waggled bushy eyebrows, clearly trying— and failing—to flirt with her.

Pen was quite sure she was gaping. How on earth did a Highlander who stumbled over something like a simple greeting manage to graduate from Cambridge? With *honors*, no less? Some miserable part of her burned in envy. She might have liked to attend university herself, though her impoverished upbringing and gender had ensured no such opportunities existed.

She knew she needed to write some of this down. Perhaps this was even a greater story than the plight of the town's businessmen or Moraig's general appeal to London tourists.

But her pencil was frozen in shock.

"Are you sure the rumors say *Cambridge?*" she asked weakly.

The butcher laughed, showing again that great gaping maw of a mouth. "Dinna take me wrong, lass. MacKenzie's not the sort to put on airs. He'll gladly raise a pint with me at the Gander, even though he lives in yon great castle."

Pen turned slowly, following the arc of McRory's hand. He was pointing to a far-off bluff, rising high in the distance with the Atlantic Ocean at its back, on top of which sat a structure of uncertain architecture but unmistakable grandeur.

"MacKenzie lives in a c-castle?" An image of the man, standing in front of the posting house like a fierce Highland warrior, swam in her mind. Surely a cave or crofter's cottage was a more appropriate dwelling for that man. The mere thought of the vista from the windows of the castle on the hill took her breath her away.

The butcher nodded like a soothsayer. "Aye. Kilmartie Castle." He shrugged as though *she* were the one lacking the intelligence here. "Where else would the heir to the Earl of Kilmartie live?"

Good heavens, the surprises kept coming, like ocean waves, determined to erode her initial middling impression of the man. Her head was spinning with the disparate images.

She tore her gaze from the castle and looked speculatively over her shoulder. The sunlight gleamed like a spotlight on MacKenzie's flexing shoulders, a lure she was finding impossible to resist. Perhaps that physique came from a willingness to work on behalf of the town, no matter how secure his own future was. He was a conundrum that demanded further exploration. She'd come to town today, notebook in hand, determined to unearth the hidden heart of this story.

Instead, it seemed she'd come closer to unearthing the hidden heart of the entire town.

"It seems as though Mr. MacKenzie is a man of many surprises," she mused, her eyes drifting appreciatively across the shirtless form of her subject. "I b-believe you must pass a series of rigorous examinations in order attend Cambridge."

"Aye, he's smart enough. But it isn't going to help him on Saturday," McRory said smugly. "We won't be tossing books, you ken." He placed his boot on the long length of larch tree lying at his feet, striking an assertive pose. "The caber weighs nigh on twelve stone. He canna throw it as far as me, I promise you that."

"Well," she said, smiling, "I look forward to seeing you both."

Pen gingerly extracted herself from Mr. McRory, leaving him in the company of his large caber and even larger ego, and then made her way toward the scaffolding. MacKenzie seemed possessed in a frenzy of work, hammering nails, one after the other, as though his very life depended on it. She looked up, extending the shade of her bonnet with a flattened palm. The overhead sun was blinding, and she squinted, trying to make out the shape of him.

"Hullo!" she called up. "MacKenzie! Might I have a word with you?"

The hammering abruptly stopped, and shortly after came a muffled curse, followed by a large, dark shape hurtling toward the earth.

He hit the ground, flat on his back, with a thump that made her teeth rattle.

"MacKenzie!" she cried, tossing her notebook aside and dropping to her knees in the dust of the street. He was heaving, eyes scrunched tight, as though the impact had startled him as much as her. Intending to calm him, she placed her hands on his chest.

His very large, very bare chest.

The slick sweat off his skin soaked through her gloves, but far from being repelled by it, she leaned over him, searching for obvious injuries. There was no blood she could see, thank goodness. At least he was still breathing, the nearly panicked rise and fall of his ribs telling her he was working for a lungful of air. The fall must have been twenty feet or more, and it was a miracle he hadn't landed on his Cambridge-educated head.

She looked up again to see a similarly bare-chested James MacKenzie shimmying down the side of the structure in a more graceful—and far safer—manner.

"Is he all right?" Pen asked, feeling a bit panicked.

Rather than showing the expected brotherly concern—though admittedly, Pen knew little about brothers—James nudged his brother with a boot, which prompted the prone giant to growl out a warning. James laughed. "Aye, I think so. He's only been struck dumb in your presence again."

"Struck d-dumb?" she echoed, confused. And what did he mean *again*?

"He's probably b-broken a rib or two," she said indignantly. "And he can't breathe. I'd scarcely expect him to be able to speak."

"*That* wee fall?" James scoffed. "God help a Highlander whose ribs aren't made of sterner stuff than that. Why, I once chased down a man bent on murder with a split skull, a knife wound to the chest, and an injured knee to slow me down."

"You dinna catch him though," MacKenzie wheezed, climbing slowly to his feet.

"Should you be standing?" Pen asked weakly, all too aware of how he towered over her.

"I am fine," he rasped and then offered a hand down to help her rise as well. She placed her hand in his, struck by the coiled strength she could feel radiating from his body as he pulled her to standing. Sterner stuff, indeed. "And Jamie-boy is only saying such things because his own ribs are made from butterfly wings."

James picked up his shirt and pulled it over his head, grinning. "Butterfly wings, aye? Well then, I suppose I'll just flutter on over to the Gander and get a cool drink." Laughing green eyes shifted to hers. "But try not to befuddle him further, Miss Tolbertson. His ribs may be fine, but perchance the fall has knocked some of the sense out of him, aye?"

MacKenzie glared at his brother's retreating back, muttering something about butterflies for brains as well. Pen looked down, hiding the smile that threatened to claim her. No, she didn't know anything about brothers. But she sensed that beneath the bickering lay affection and even respect, and she was none too worried about MacKenzie's head, after she'd felt the steady strength in his hand.

Seeing a remaining shirt lying in the shade of the scaffolding, Pen bent down and picked it up. But instead of proffering it like the peace offering she had intended, some perverse, devilish instinct made her hold it behind her back.

"What did your b-brother mean: not to *befuddle* you *further?*" she asked. She hoped it meant what she imagined. Because it was becoming more and more difficult not to stare at the flexing muscles in this man's shoulders, and she had a mind to indulge in a bit more research before this little trip was over.

MacKenzie turned toward her and shook his head. "Dinna pay him any mind. He's daft."

"I thought he was a solicitor," she teased.

"He's a *daft* solicitor," MacKenzie amended. He looked at her, almost sheepishly. "You…ah…said you wished to have a word with me?"

Pen searched for an opening—any opening—that might further the conversation, now that she had pulled him from his work. "I understand you're to enter the caber competition?" He nodded warily. "Mr. McRory implied he is going to throw it farther than you." She paused, searching his broad face for a reaction. "Do you have anything to say in response?"

He treated her to a slow, spreading kind of grin that made him look suddenly boyish. "Aye. McRory might believe he can toss it farther." He leaned in, and she could smell the sharp, healthy tang of hard-earned sweat from his body. "But 'tis not the length of a man's stick that matters, you ken. It's his aim."

Pen gasped, her thoughts immediately flying to things that had nothing to do with cabers and everything to do with warm, sweaty, shirtless bodies.

Had he meant to be so suggestive?

But no…the tips of his ears were reddening, as if he had only now realized how his words might be interpreted. "I mean, the caber is not only judged on the length of the throw, but how straight. It must go end over and fall in a straight line to acquire the maximum points. I've been watching McRory from atop the scaffolding, and he's none too straight with his aim, aye?"

She nodded, though a dangerous part of her wanted to discuss the length and relative aim of MacKenzie's stick. She cleared her throat, not wanting the conversation to end just yet. "I've another question for you, if you d-don't mind. I've a wish to see inside Kilmartie Castle. I understand you're the man to help me with that."

He tensed. "Did McRory say something he oughtn't have?"

"That you are the heir to the Earl of Kilmartie?" Pen raised a brow. "He might have mentioned something of that n-nature."

"The butcher's as daft as my brother." Brown eyes narrowed down on her. "The town loves a bit of gossip, as I am sure you are discovering. But it's harmless, really. Part of Moraig's charm. You shouldn't pay it any mind."

"Like the crodh mara?"

"Aye. Very much like that."

"Well, I rather enjoyed meeting your water cattle." Pen smiled sweetly, though what she felt was a bit more complicated. "So it stands to reason I might enjoy the c-castle as well." She leaned in, his shirt still clasped tightly behind her back. "And you *did* assure me you would show me anything I wished," she added.

He stared at her a moment, as though surprised she would be so frank. He seemed to be sidestepping any mention of that memorable night, but the same devil that had caused her to hide his shirt made her want to remind him of their kiss at every opportunity.

Finally, he scrubbed a hand across his brow. "Aye. I did. So come to the castle around seven o'clock tonight then. Bring your sister and Cameron, as well. I'll invite James and his wife, and we can make a dinner of it."

Pen nodded. She was pleased he had agreed so easily, though she was disappointed to hear they would have an audience. She'd hoped to have his undivided attention.

Something made her want to dig deeper here. It wasn't only the story. It was the man himself. She felt as though she were uncovering him, one secret at a time. "McRory also said you graduated from Cambridge." At his frown, she plunged on. "It seems like you might be trying to hide some facts from me, MacKenzie. But as I said, I am an excellent journalist. I'll sort out the t-truth eventually, with or without you."

"I have no doubts about your capabilities as a journalist, but I am not hiding, Miss Tolbertson." What might have been a glower darkened his face. "It's only that the focus of your story ought to be the town. *They* are the ones in need. I prefer to stay in the background and help where I can, and my own situation has nothing to do with it."

"Organizing the entire event is scarcely j-just helping where you can," she pointed out, though she couldn't help but feel a swell of respect for a man so determined to put the town first. With her free hand, she gestured to the wood structure that had so recently handed him his downfall. "*Look* at you. You're risking life and limb to b-build this for Moraig." She paused, blinking up at the massive set of wood. "Although, what *is* this, if I might ask?"

"'Tis a music stage," he said, a bit less gruffly. "We've pipers and musicians planned. Music is as much a part of our tradition here as the games." He hesitated. "Mayhap you'll consent to share a dance with me, Miss Tolbertson?"

"Perhaps." She tried to ignore the sudden leap of her heart, which was all too willing to agree with anything that might send her into this man's strong arms again. Her fingers curled around the bit of cotton she still held behind her back. "*If* you'll put on a shirt."

He looked down, clearly startled by the reminder. "Ach, my brother," he muttered, looking around on the ground. "He's taken my shirt, it seems. Daft, I tell you. Meddlesome, too."

Pen laughed. Time for the game she had started to end.

Or perhaps, it was time for it to begin?

She'd kissed him, of course, and he'd kissed her back, but she hadn't precisely made her hopes clear. She brought his shirt out slowly from behind her back, dangling it from one gloved finger. He looked at her in what might have been panic.

Or perhaps befuddlement.

"You were hiding my clothes?" His brows pulled down in confusion as he accepted the shirt from her. His fingers crumpled in the fabric, but he looked at a loss to know what to do with it.

Ah, there was the return of the bumbling giant.

She was discovering she enjoyed being able to pull it from his university-educated skull.

"I was merely enjoying *all* the views Moraig has to offer, MacKenzie," she answered, though her unaccustomed boldness meant her cheeks felt as though someone had held them too close to a candle. "Perhaps you might show me more later?"

"The castle. As we agreed." His ears reddened even more. "And I…ah…thought we agreed you might call me 'William.'"

She bent and scooped up her notebook, dusting it off. "I don't think of you as a William."

Couldn't, in fact. In her mind, he was simply *MacKenzie*.

She straightened and met his gaze, willing her words to behave properly for once. She concentrated on every syllable, determined to get it right. "But please, do call me 'Pen.'" A smile that was anything but serene claimed her lips. "A man who's kissed me in the moonlight might have earned the p-privilege, hmm?"

CHAPTER FIVE

"She thinks I'm an idiot." William frowned at James and David Cameron, who were standing in the library, glasses of port in hand.

The interminable dinner might be finished, but he was unfortunately still dressed in the sort of formal attire that made his feet itch and his neck feel as though hands were closing in, choking the life out of him. Christ, even the plaid was better than this.

But guests for dinner at Kilmartie Castle meant manners, and manners meant neckties.

"No, *I'm* the one who thinks you are an idiot," David Cameron chuckled, swirling the port in his glass. "Caroline and her sister think your idea for the Highland Games is a brilliant opportunity for the town."

William should have felt like smiling. It was good to hear of Caroline's approval. She was a fine woman, one who spoke her mind and managed her own opinions. She had turned David Cameron around for the better, when it had once seemed he'd been bound for little beyond a life of dissolution.

But unfortunately, William felt less concerned with Caroline's approval than her sister's. Pen didn't *act* as though she thought the games were a good idea.

For some reason, it mattered, and not only because of her role in his plans for Moraig.

"I was given the impression during dinner she was still forming an opinion," he muttered, staring down into his drink. In point of fact, she had asked everyone at the table their views, scribbling each response down in her notebook, but she had not publicly divulged her own thoughts on the matter.

"You refer to Penelope?" Cameron asked.

William looked up. "You don't call her 'Pen'?"

A fair brow shot up. "Do *you* call her 'Pen'?"

William's collar suddenly felt even tighter, though it was already cinched as tight as a miser's purse. "I...ah...that is... She's invited me to use her given name," he admitted.

"And yet, her given name is *Penelope*," Cameron mused. Blue eyes narrowed in William's direction. "Only Caroline calls her 'Pen.'"

James burst out laughing and slapped William on the back, which had the misfortune of rattling the ribs still sore from his earlier fall. "Perhaps she was more impressed by your cattle than you thought," James chuckled. "Though I might have chosen something different as tonight's main course. She looked a wee bit upset when Father proudly told her it was kyloe beef."

"I only showed her the breeding stock," William protested. The cows he'd shown Pen were far too valuable to grace a dinner plate. But there was still no doubt he'd felt like a bloody bounder when her eyes had widened and she'd set her fork down firmly.

"Well, have a care. I'll not have it said you were taking advantage of Caroline's sister." Cameron's initial scowl shifted to a grin. "Although, did you really pretend your cattle were *fairies?* Good God, man. I nearly burst a gut when she told us about that. Have you lost your bollocks completely?"

William shrugged off their mirth. He was used to this sort of ribbing, though he was more often on the giving end of it than the receiving end. He refilled his glass, wondering if it might give him the same kind of courage he'd found two nights ago in the whisky. Damn it, what was wrong with him? He'd been a silent, fumbling fool during dinner, and now the moment he opened his mouth, something ridiculous came out. He'd not meant to call her "Pen" in public, and *certainly* not in front of Cameron.

Perhaps he needed to be drunk around her for proper conversation. He drained his glass in a convulsive swallow. It was a sacrifice he was willing to make again.

"Well, chin up," James said, finishing the rest of his glass as well and then turning toward the door. "You'll have another chance to humiliate yourself soon enough. Time to join the fairer sex in the drawing room."

"Aye," Cameron snickered as they made their way into the room filled with feminine laughter. "Perhaps you should offer to show her your fairy kittens, next."

"Fairy k-kittens?" Pen said, looking up with sharp interest from the settee.

William's attention arrowed in on her as though loosened from a bow. The sight of her felt as though someone had kicked him, and not in entirely pleasant places. Tonight she looked a proper lady, blond hair piled high, a gown of lovely blue silk highlighting her delicate curves. *Curves he'd recently held against him.*

And dear God, she had little Lizzie on her lap.

Though the dinner had been formal, the tone in the drawing room was decidedly less so. William's mother, the countess, had insisted on seeing her granddaughter, and so James's daughter had been fetched down from the nursery and was being passed around the drawing room and properly fussed over. At five months old, Lizzie was a sweet thing, with blue eyes and pink cheeks she'd inherited from Georgette, and a pair of healthy lungs that she'd no doubt acquired from James.

There were times when William could not help but battle a bit of envy at his brother's good fortune. Seeing this child he loved sitting on Pen's lap made that envy shift into something more defined.

Want. He wanted what his brother had. A wife, a child. Happiness.

Looking around, he realized he was the only male in the room who didn't have those essential things. James had found Georgette. Even David Cameron—who probably didn't deserve anything beyond a swift kick in the bollocks—had found love, the gentle swell of his wife's belly demonstrating his own state of contentedness.

And with a startled bit of insight, William realized as he looked at Penelope Tolbertson holding this small, blond-haired baby on her lap, he might find those things with this woman. It wasn't even an outrageous thought. He was thirty-five years old. The expectations of his future title demanded he marry, after all, and Moraig wasn't exactly brimming with potential mates.

Why *not* Penelope Tolbertson? She was beautiful. She was intelligent.

She was *here.*

And there was no denying she made his heart race, quite happily so.

She was also still waiting for his answer. He cleared his throat, hoping the port had worked its magic. "Er…'tis just a story about kittens. For wee Lizzie." He gestured to his niece, who began to bounce happily on Pen's lap at the sound of her name. "She's too small for cattle, aye?"

Pen smiled up at him, her blue eyes crinkling about the edges, and he wanted to dive into that smile and never let go. No one he'd met in Moraig or beyond had ever stirred his fancy in quite this way. But as he mulled over this startling, tempting new idea, he was also struck by an almost painful awareness of how impossible it was.

She lived in London and was clearly committed to her position as a reporter. He was devoted to Moraig and had organized the games because he wanted to ensure the prosperity of the town where he intended to spend his life.

He *needed* her to return to London with a story to convince others to come.

Otherwise, it was all for naught.

As the men took their seats, Pen stole a surreptitious look at the one man among them whose appearance made her heart thump faster.

She'd been seated opposite MacKenzie at dinner, so she'd been able to look all she wanted—and she was coming to understand she wanted a good deal. But once again, though he'd certainly been a pleasure to look upon, he'd proven a poor conversationalist, reverting to grunts and fumbles. He didn't resemble anything close to the silver-tongued man who'd kissed her senseless and made her believe in fairies two nights ago.

But Pen was an expert in the matter of tangled responses, and she was beginning to understand that more than dim wits lay beneath MacKenzie's mumbles.

He hesitated only with her. She'd observed him carry on a pleasant enough conversation with her sister, Caroline, and he'd spoken easily and warmly with Georgette. When his opinions were directed to the table at large, they were well formed and educated.

In fact, Pen was ashamed of herself for reaching such a quick judgment of his intelligence before. She, of all people, understood what it was like to be measured by the ease of one's words and found wanting.

"How do you find the town, Miss Tolbertson?" Georgette smiled, holding out her hands for her daughter.

Pen dutifully passed the babe on to its mother, leaving the child with a quick kiss on the top of her fair head and a discreet inhalation to preserve the precious scent. "'Tis lovely, though in truth I've only seen a b-bit of it." She hesitated. "B-both times I've come to Moraig, I've stayed with Caroline, you see, so my forays into town have been limited."

"Perhaps you ought to stay a night or two in town," James suggested, smiling down at his wife and daughter. He reached out a finger, which Lizzie grabbed, gurgling happily. "After all, there's a room still held at the Blue Gander, waiting to impress our reporter up from London."

Pen blinked in confusion. "Why would they still b-be holding the room?" she asked. She'd been very clear on the matter of her lodging.

There was a moment of awkward silence. Everyone in the room looked at each other, as though gauging the moment and the appropriate response. And then Georgette sighed, almost apologetically. "William personally had a room in the inn refurbished for the reporter we expected and then paid in advance for a week's use of it. The innkeeper is still holding it."

Pen sidled a surprised glance toward MacKenzie, who looked irritated by the disclosure. She recalled his stumbled confusion the day she had met him, how she'd presumed his insistence on walking her to the Blue Gander to have been the result of misplaced masculine superiority.

She regretted being so quick to dismiss his idea now.

Her impressions of the town were clearly very important to him, but he had bowed to her wishes and not breathed a word of his efforts. Her respect swelled another notch.

"I might enjoy staying at the B-blue Gander during the games," she admitted. "In order to get a more authentic feel for the town, as a tourist would." She looked up at her sister. "Would you mind, Caro? Only for a night or two?"

Caroline smiled. "No, I know how important this story is to you." She curled a hand around her growing belly and shared a warm look with her husband. "You should do whatever you need to get it right." And by the look they exchanged, it seemed Caroline and her husband might make the most of the bit of privacy.

Pen turned to MacKenzie, suddenly aware that out of everyone in the room, they were the only ones without a match. Her stomach did a queer flip at the thought. Did he feel it too, this sense of destiny? "Will you show me the room there tomorrow?"

He swallowed and cast about his eyes, as though in search of a savior.

"You d-did offer to show me anything I wished," she reminded him, a bit peeved he had to think so hard about it.

Brown eyes met hers slowly. "Aye. I did." He nodded gruffly. "Tomorrow, then. Six o'clock. I'll arrange it with the innkeeper."

Pen smiled her thanks and then stood up, her skirts falling decisively about her feet. The picture of perfect gentlemen, the men stood dutifully as well. She knew what she was about to do might be viewed as forward, but she hoped the others in the room would presume her request was for the article she planned to write.

She'd wrangled this invitation to Kilmartie Castle in the hopes of procuring a few moments alone with MacKenzie, but so far it had been an ordinary—and crowded—sort of dinner party. In fact, he seemed determined to put an even greater distance between them, and she was determined to see it reversed. She only had a few more days in town, and she didn't want to waste them dancing around what could be. "And would you also show me the view from the front lawn tonight, Mr. MacKenzie?" she asked, pulling her notebook from her reticule as a sort of cover. "It seems as though it should be a spectacular s-sunset."

"Sunset?" MacKenzie said hoarsely, not moving toward her in the slightest.

She inclined her head and waved her notebook. "Research, you know."

There was a beat of silence, where he seemed to be considering how to tell her no.

But then James grabbed William by the arm and propelled him toward the door. "He'd be happy to, Miss Tolbertson." James grinned. "Capital idea, a bit of research."

MacKenzie scowled as he shook his brother free and then grimly offered her his arm. She accepted it and then tried to temper the tilt of her heart as he escorted her from the room. They walked down an endless hallway where their footsteps echoed and scores of Earls of Kilmartie stared down from the wall. She'd thought he would say something. *Anything.* After all, he'd kissed her, only two nights ago. They were something past mere acquaintances.

But he seemed determined to show her the sunset and not a single thing more.

Finally they stepped out of the front doors on to the lawn, and Pen drew in a startled breath, her fingers curling into the solid strength of his arm. This afternoon, when McRory had pointed out the castle to her, she'd imagined the view from its lawn would be magnificent.

She considered now whether *staggering* might be a more appropriate word choice.

The lawn swept down to the edge of a cliff, shimmering against a kaleidoscope sky. The clouds seemed set on fire and all too happy to burn. She could see white-capped surf in the distance and, as the coast curved out of sight, magnificent stone cliffs plunging to the sea.

"It's…incredible," she whispered, shading her eyes with her notebook and trying to take it all in. She was a confident writer, but how on earth could she be expected to describe something like this in the space of a newspaper article?

"Aye," he agreed stiffly. "I never grow tired of it."

"I c-can't imagine you would." She tried to write a few notes down but found the wind was too strong, fluttering the pages under her hand. Moreover, she found she didn't want to take her eyes from the view a second longer than was necessary.

Sighing, she shoved the notebook back in her reticule.

Perhaps she was spending too much time with it anyway. Wasn't the point of the experience to see things as a tourist would?

"I've been thinking more about the things McRory told you today," MacKenzie said, his voice a rumble over the wind. "'Tis fine if you mention the castle as a historical site, but I'd appreciate if you dinna mention me your article."

Pen shifted her eyes to him and found the view every bit as moving as the one on the horizon. He was staring out at the cliff as though seeing it for the first time. The amber light softened his features, and the breeze tumbled strands of dark hair about his forehead. She could see hints of silver at his temples, and she imagined having the freedom and the permission to run her fingers through it.

What would he do if she kissed him again, this time with the sun on their faces?

"But…why?" she asked, truly curious about his answer. She was beginning to think MacKenzie was quite possibly the most important piece of it all.

"I dinna take it for granted, you ken." He raised his hand, sweeping it wide. "The title, the castle, any of it. We were not raised to this. My father only came to be earl by a series of unforeseen events." His gaze pulled to hers, and she was startled to see an almost pleading look in his eyes. "I suppose what I am trying to say is that I intend this opportunity to help the town, not myself. I've already been given more than I need."

Pen felt a spreading warmth in her chest. "I think I understand," she said softly. "And I won't mention you, if you d-do not wish me to." At his nod of thanks, she smiled. "I only hope they appreciate what you are doing for them. You have g-gone to a great deal of trouble to impress me, arranging this room at the Blue Gander. I am looking forward to seeing it tomorrow."

In fact, the thought of having MacKenzie alone, in a room with a bed and four walls and a lock on the door, made the breath grow short in her lungs.

She imagined he blanched somewhat. "About the Gander," he said, shaking his head, "I think it might be better to have James show the room to you."

Pen's lips firmed. Why was he trying so hard to avoid her? She was admittedly inexperienced in the ways of men, but every nuanced gesture, every mangled word, told her MacKenzie was attracted to her.

"I think you are the b-better choice," she told him. "In fact, I quite insist on it."

Finally, he nodded, but he did not look happy about it.

She refused to feel a twinge of guilt at his clear reluctance. What would it hurt to see where this went? She would be no future burden to him, had no designs to trap him in marriage. She would go back to London with a lovely memory, and he would remain in Moraig with…well, with whatever men had after spending a night in the arms of a woman.

It was all a bit jumbled in her head.

And she had every intention of unjumbling it before this trip was over.

CHAPTER SIX

Penelope arrived early to stage the scene of her own seduction.

She stepped inside the room the innkeeper showed her, absorbing the details with the eye of someone who would faithfully report her findings later. Lace curtains fluttered against the open window, and beyond them she could hear the pleasant sounds of conversation out on the street. There was fresh paint on the walls, a lovely soft blue that made her regret not having stayed here from the start.

She set her bag down and smiled at the anxious innkeeper. "It is quite lovely."

The man pulled a kerchief from his pocket and mopped the top of his balding head. "Well, at the Blue Gander, we pride ourselves on running a clean, respectable establishment. You might mention in your article that the maid, Sally, is instructed to provide the guests anything they might want. They have only to ask."

Pen suppressed a giggle, recalling the exchange she had overheard several nights ago. Sally's offer hadn't sounded very respectable to her, but perhaps it might appeal to a certain kind of tourist. Namely, the *male* tourists.

But she nodded encouragingly, wrote a few things down in her notebook, and then shooed the innkeeper on, determined to have a moment alone to collect her thoughts before MacKenzie arrived and sent them scattering to the winds again.

She paused a moment, listening to the open window with a cocked ear. The games started tomorrow morning, and already the town's population had begun to swell in anticipation. By the conversations she could hear swirling on the street, it seemed half the town was betting on Mr. McRory to win the famed caber toss.

The other half were betting on William MacKenzie.

She counted herself among the latter, but not only in the matter of cabers.

She smoothed a hand over the bed's beautiful coverlet, a patchwork of bright colors embroidered with a Celtic cross. The room felt bright and new, but it also held what appeared to be Caledonian artifacts on the bureau, illustrating the rich history of the land and its people. She paused, fingering a small statue. Clearly, a good deal of thought and effort had been put into this. As a reporter and a tourist, Pen could appreciate the careful perfection of the room.

As a woman bent on seduction, however, it was not quite right.

So she shut the window and pulled the lace curtains closed against the early-evening sun, until the room was bathed only in a lovely, dim light. She turned back the beautiful embroidered coverlet on the bed and plumped the pillows. She opened her valise and pulled out a small bottle of vinegar and a sponge, taking the hopeful precaution she'd read about but had never thought to need. Thank goodness Moraig wasn't so rustic as to lack a chemist shop.

Should she change into something more…accessible?

But no, her night rails were plain cotton, hardly the stuff of lustful fantasies. She had not packed her bag in London intending to seek out this experience, and she'd never seen the need for a trousseau. Until she'd met MacKenzie, she'd never met a man who'd made her regret her choice of sleeping garments.

She unfastened the top buttons of her bodice and then studied her reflection critically in the washstand mirror. The shadowed vee between her breasts was just visible, and so she loosened another button. It would not do to go into battle unarmed, particularly when her opponent seemed so reluctant to engage in the sort of skirmish she sought.

She was paler than she would like, and she did not want MacKenzie to think she was nervous. She pinched her cheeks and then pulled the pins from her hair, one by one, until the warm, heavy coils fell about her shoulders.

She studied her reflection again. Yes, that was better.

She looked ready to be ravished.

Unless she'd made the room too dark for him to notice her efforts…

She was halfway to the window, intending to open the curtains again, when the sound of boots on the threshold froze her in place. She turned slowly, her heart like a hammer in her chest.

He stood in the doorway, his big shoulders nearly filling the space to completion. He looked confused as his eyes dropped to her bodice, a long, slow slide of perusal that made her skin burn in anticipation. She laced her fingers in front of her in a bid to control their trembling.

"C-come inside, MacKenzie," she somehow found the courage to say.

After a moment's hesitation, he did, placing his hat on the bureau next to the artifacts. "I was surprised when the innkeeper said you were already here. I thought we had agreed to six o'clock."

"I wanted a moment to see the r-room alone. Research, you know."

"Aye." His voice sounded hoarse. "I know how you like your research." His eyes lingered on her unbound hair, and a stark look of want settled over his face. "You…ah…look as though you are ready to take a wee nap. Should I come back later?"

"*No.*" The word escaped her lips more harshly than she'd intended. She calmed herself with a carefully indrawn breath. "That is, I am not t-tired." She moved toward the door and was dismayed to see him edge away.

For heaven's sake. She was not going to bite him.

Unless he wanted her to.

She reached the door just as he reached the bed. He scratched his head, looking very much like the bumbling beast who had greeted her outside the posting house. "Is… er…everything in the room to your liking?"

She shut the door and locked it. "*Now* it is."

"Miss Tolbertson—"

"Pen. As we agreed."

She stepped toward him, and as the bed was at his back, he really had nowhere to go. He shuffled an uncomfortable moment, enduring her determined advance, his dark eyes everywhere and nowhere on her skin. "Cameron says only your sister is permitted to call you 'Pen.' That others, when invited to do so, call you 'Penelope.'"

That made her stop a moment. Was it true? She'd never taken the time to think on it. And moreover, what did that mean? If William MacKenzie was naught but a fling, why had she invited him to address her so intimately? There was something about him—his eagerness to please, his devotion to town and family—that engendered as much by way of friendship as seduction. She shook her head, trying to clear it of that thought.

She had not staged the room to procure only his friendship.

She took another step. "You invited me to call *you* 'William.'"

"And yet you do not." He pulled a hand through his dark hair, as though trying to settle his nerves. He cast a hand to the staged bed. "What are we doing here, Pen? If not a nap, what, precisely, do you want from me?"

She was nearly on him now, and the hand he had just pulled through his hair reached out as though to stop her. But he was very tall, and she was not, and the gesture had the fortunate effect of placing his fingers very close to her waiting breasts. She could feel the calloused rasp of his fingers against the sensitive skin she had exposed and imagined she could feel the acceleration of his pulse as he touched her. She placed her hand over his, pressing it into her flesh.

"I w-want you to show me this," she whispered.

Brown eyes burned down at her, delivering a message that was nearly the opposite of reluctance. And yet, his hand stayed rigid against her body, a warning and perhaps a plea. "You play a dangerous game, lass. I'm a man who wants you fiercely. It is not easy to remain a gentleman when you look at me so."

His admission made her heart leap wildly. *He wanted her.* She was not imagining the tension that hummed between them. And where there was want, there was hope.

"Then d-don't remain a gentleman." She stared at his mouth, which looked ready to devour her at a single word. "I am t-twenty-six, MacKenzie. A stammering spinster, with no intention or d-desire to marry." She pushed against his hand and leaned in, going up on her toes, until her lips hovered only a few inches from his. "But that does not mean I do not want—do not *deserve*—to know something of life."

His fingers seemed to soften against her skin. "You do not have to be a spinster," he said softly, in his stomach-turning brogue. "Christ, Pen, you've passion enough for five women. You could have a husband and see that passion met every day if you wished." His lips lowered a fraction of an inch, an unfulfilled promise she could still not quite reach. "And do not use your stammer as an excuse. Any gentleman would count himself fortunate to have you."

That startled her enough to make her blink. *Was* she using her stammer as an excuse? Certainly, the men of Brighton had considered her an object to mock, rather than kiss. Had she pushed away all thoughts of love and marriage because her desire for self-sufficiency had demanded it or simply because they had seemed out of reach?

With her pulse so heavy in her ears, it was hard to sort out which had come first.

"I d-do not wish to take a husband," she said, almost desperately now. "I enjoy my independence, and I won't b-barter my body for the purpose of procuring a protector I do not need." She pulled his hand lower, until it was pressed more fully against the swell of her breast. "I *want* this. I am bound to d-discover it eventually. But you are the only one who has ever made the breath catch in my throat, MacKenzie. I want this experience to be with you, not someone else."

His eyes narrowed, as though imagining—and disapproving—of the thought of her doing this with someone else.

She licked her lips. "And you *d-did* say you would show me whatever I wished."

With a growl, his lips descended on hers, and then she was pulled into the dark heat of him, the kiss blissful and brutal and beautiful, all at once.

And oh, dear heavens, how this man could kiss. His mouth moved against hers, tongue stroking her own in a wicked hint of promise. She wrapped her arms around his neck, wanting to be only closer. They fell backward onto the bed, her body stretched against his hard length, their mouths still joined in battle. He tasted of salt and outdoors and the merest hint of tooth powder, and the scrape of his chin against her cheek was its own kind of pleasure.

She regretted, then, not having changed into her night rail, because if she had, they'd be halfway closer to where she wanted to be.

She gave her hands permission to roam, making short work of his necktie as they kissed and then moving lower. As her fingers splayed over his broad, hard chest, she could feel the coiled strength lying in wait beneath the linen of his shirt.

She ripped several buttons free from his collar in frustration as she slipped her hand inside, wanting to be closer still.

But with a muffled groan, he broke off their kiss and shifted their bodies, putting more space between them. She wanted to pant her objection, pull him back into the kiss, but she stilled as the change in their positions began to register in her quivering thoughts.

Suddenly *she* was the one on her back.

He had taken control.

And he was rearing over her, looking every inch the wild Highlander.

She waited for him to fall on her, waited for the ravishment she'd been hoping for. Instead he lifted a hand and rubbed his knuckles against her cheek, almost tenderly, though his features seemed strained with the effort of holding back. "If we are going to do this, lass, we'll take it a bit slower, aye?"

Pen caught her lower lip in her teeth and somehow found the sense to nod. He appeared to be agreeing with her proposition, praise the temptation gods. She did not want to do or say anything that might send him running now.

He dipped his head, pressing his warm mouth to the hollow at the base of her throat. She sucked in a breath, surprised at the gentle heat of his touch but willing to follow his lead, as long as he did not stop. Her entire body was trembling now, and at her core there was a delicious, spreading heat that made her feel a bit like molten wax, waiting to be shaped into what he would make her.

She was still in too many clothes, the ridiculous froth of skirts and crinolines making her want to gnash her teeth. But the flash of air on heated skin that told her the buttons of her bodice were now being completely undone. She acknowledged that perhaps there was a certain delicious anticipation to be found in the unwrapping.

A wicked grin claimed his face as he took in her simple corset. "It laces in the front," was all he said.

Pen's cheeks heated, knowing her undergarments were nothing close to the height of fashion. "It is easier to d-dress without a maid."

He went to work unlacing it and parted the stiffened fabric almost reverently. "Praise the saints for your independence then, lass, because you are easier to undress as well." The low tenor of his approval sent a snaking down her spine.

He pulled the straps of her chemise down and then stared down at her, no longer moving.

No longer *breathing*.

Pen squirmed, but he stilled her with a hand. "Lie still, lass, and let me look at you."

She would have rather he just kissed her again, but she held herself motionless, sensing this was somehow part of the process, though looking and touching had not been mentioned in *any* of the books she'd read on the subject.

Finally, he began to swirl a hand over her aching, greedy skin. "I wanted this first sight of you for a memory. You are too beautiful for words."

Pen swallowed, though his hands were wreaking havoc on her senses. *Memory*, he'd said, as though acknowledging that what lay between them was temporary at best.

But it didn't feel temporary. It felt…portentous.

As though she was about to be changed forever.

And then his head was lowering to her breast, and he was drawing her nipple into the heat of his mouth, and she gasped at the unexpected waves of feeling rolling through her. How was that possible? His mouth was there, but she felt it lower. Deeper.

Stupid books and their scientific explanations.

She closed her eyes and tipped her head back, drowning in the feel of all he was doing to her. He was a generous lover, paying as much attention to one breast as the other, his hands roaming, touching, until she was panting with need. He loosened her skirts, dragged them free, and then worked his hands and mouth *up* her body, leaving a wake of devastation and longing as he moved on to new places. She let him.

No, she *begged* him, scarcely able to believe the pants and cries that echoed softly in her ears were her own.

Gently, he parted her thighs, and she could feel the moist heat of his breath as he kissed first one trembling limb and then the other. And then his fingers were *there*, in a spot that made her hips buck upward from the bed. A gasp of surprise wrenched from her lips.

She thought she'd understood her body. The process outlined in the books she had read.

How unbelievably wrong she had been.

He responded with a low, throaty chuckle. "Perhaps I need to revise my assessment, lass. You've passion enough for ten women, I think."

And then, still pressing against that secret, mind-stealing spot, he slipped his fingers inside her. As her body stretched to meet the demand, Pen was launched into a different sort of feeling, one that seemed to come from within.

But abruptly, he stilled, his fingers still deep inside her. "You've put in a sponge?" he whispered, his voice hoarse with disbelief.

She nodded, cheeks burning. She'd naively imagined the precaution would be her secret, but she'd not counted on fingers as part of the process. "I d-do not want to risk a child, not when I'm to return to London in two days." She lifted herself on her elbows and risked a look down at him. He looked shaken by his discovery. "I've read a good d-deal on the subject," she reassured him. "I know what I am about in that regard."

He swallowed. "So you mean to go through with all of it then?"

"Do you not?" She felt herself blush, which was an odd response, given that his fingers were still embedded in that most intimate part of her. "I want all of it, MacKenzie. All of *you*."

And for once, her words did not fail her.

Miraculously, he nodded. She pressed her head back against the pillow and gave herself up to it. To *him*. His fingers seemed to know just where to press to make the breath catch in her throat and her body writhe in anticipation.

And then she was there, teetering on the edge of something unknown.

"MacKenzie," she gasped. "This feeling...I do not...I c-cannot..."

"Trust me, *mo ghraidh*."

The sound of that whispered endearment was enough to send her over. Her body exploded beneath his fingers, a shower of sparks and feeling that seemed to reverberate through every inch of her. It drew on endlessly, and then, with a small cry of relief, it was gone, tendrils of want and feeling the only thing left in its wake.

She felt…boneless. Surely there was a more sophisticated word for it, but right now, in the haze of such pleasure, she could not think beyond the simplicity of the word.

And then he was looming over her, and dimly she became aware that somehow he had shed his clothing. Dark eyes met hers, a fierce question in their depths. "Last chance for regrets, Pen. We can stop here and count ourselves fortunate to have had the moment."

"No regrets," she breathed. She shook her head and wrapped her legs around his broad frame. "If you stop now, you will have only given me half the experience."

He buried his face in her neck, and she could feel the near desperate tension in his shoulders. He exhaled, a shuddering sign of his own internal battle. "I hope you know what you think you want, lass."

And then he was piercing her, and it *hurt*, but it was done, and she was glad.

Somehow, though he was undoubtedly a large sort of man, it all fit.

At last, the book had gotten it right.

She breathed in, once, twice. The pain began to subside, leaving only a delicious feeling of fullness in its place. He began to move, gently at first, and she realized with a small jolt of surprise there was more pleasure to be had here.

He cupped her head in his big hands, holding her close and kissing her deeply as they moved, slowly at first, then faster. She was caught up in the storm he kindled, feeling his body press into her core, and all too soon she was tipping over that edge once more, crying her release into his mouth, her pleasure too fierce to contain. He followed her over, his own voiced release captured by their kiss, her name a beautiful echo on his lips.

And then she was being gathered against him, held tight. A feeling like shared contentment stole over her, languid bones and loosened skin.

What on earth had just happened? She didn't feel ravished.

She felt cherished.

She'd set out to seduce him, but somehow the tables had been turned, and she was left with the sense that something had changed between them. She turned her face into his chest, tasting the sweat from his skin, feeling the crisp brush of hair against her cheek.

She was afraid to stay here, but she was equally afraid to leave.

"What does *mo ghraidh* mean, MacKenzie?" she asked quietly, fearful of the answer and yet determined to know.

She felt his arms tighten around her. "It means 'my darling.'"

She fell silent, processing the intensity of the word. It felt…*right*.

And that terrified her.

His breath ruffled her hair. "And do you think you might finally call me 'William,' lass? I'm the man who's just tupped you senseless." He pulled back, just enough to grin down at her sheepishly. "I think I might have earned the privilege, aye?"

CHAPTER SEVEN

He was an idiot.

A well-swived idiot, but an idiot nonetheless.

Yesterday William had fully intended to stop after he'd delivered Pen's pleasure. He'd intended to be a gentleman, of sorts. Instead, her whispered pleas for the entirety of the experience had quite turned his plans inside out. He was unable to deny her anything.

And had there ever been a sweeter surrender?

They'd made love again and fallen asleep near midnight, flushed and happy, tangled in the bedclothes. Some desperate part of his soul argued it was a good thing. He *liked* this woman. Possibly even loved her, though they'd known each other only a few days. Could see himself marrying her, so easily. But if William insisted on fixing their predicament with marriage—as his sensibilities told him he should—she would only hate him for trying to strip her of her modern notion of independence.

How could he think to bind her to him—to Moraig—when her heart so clearly lay in her profession and the path she had chosen for herself?

But if he let her go back to London, he would forever be a man who'd ruined an innocent. A very well-read and adventurous innocent, but an innocent, nonetheless. And he'd be left to muddle on in Moraig, with no hope for his own future.

He'd left her sleeping, just before dawn. He'd wanted to stay, to prolong the mirage of happiness another minute, another hour. But duties called.

And so he'd taken one last look. Her hair had been spread like a gold curtain across her pillow. He'd buried his nose in those fragrant tresses one last time, in lieu of a kiss that would almost certainly wake her with the force of his hunger.

And then he'd gone to work, knowing the town needed him.

The devil of it was everything was going well. By all accounts, the Highland Games he had worked so hard to organize were a success. Several hundred clansmen were in attendance, and everyone appeared to be having a marvelous time. The morning's *maide leisg* competition had drawn a raucous crowd, and the afternoon's stone put had produced a new record in the region. More to the point, Moraig's vendors were set up around the edge of the field and were doing a brisk business in meat pies, ale, and pastries.

He ought to be pleased, happy. The town's economy had gotten a much-needed boost, and if all went well with Pen's story in the *Times*, Moraig's future as a tourist destination seemed assured. Instead, he felt unsure. Miserable. Because he didn't want only one night with Pen.

He wanted a lifetime.

Even as he'd shaken hands and welcomed clansmen, he'd felt lost, wondering what she was doing and what she was thinking. Had he left her happy? Satisfied? Wanting more?

He'd caught a few glimpses of her during the day, always speaking to people, always taking notes. And now she was here, at the caber toss.

But she wasn't looking at him. She was looking at McRory.

And he wanted to smash something at the sight.

The late-afternoon sun was drawing sweat from the competitors but did not seem to be dampening the enthusiasm of the crowd in the slightest. The caber toss, the last scheduled event, was already underway, and William had drawn the last toss. But he didn't watch the other contestants, searching for clues he might use for a win.

How could he when his eyes refused to leave Pen?

The sight of her at work sent his stomach twisting in knots. She didn't belong to him, not in any sense of the word. She was her own person, refusing to conform to the usual constraints of society and propriety. Worse, by the very nature of this interview with McRory, she was proving her intentions. She was here as a reporter, and her departure was coming all too soon.

McRory's name was finally called, and a din of approval swept through the crowd. Always a town favorite—and built like a bloody draft horse—he waved to the crowd, grinning broadly. Final wagers were made, and shouts of encouragement were tossed his way.

Pen did not join the crowd.

Instead, she stepped closer to William, though she did not look at him.

The butcher picked up the caber as though it weighed no more than kindling. He heaved it higher, then higher still, until only the last bit of it rested against a shoulder.

"Mr. McRory seems in fine form," came her low, melodic voice. "You might have some d-difficulty here today, MacKenzie."

"Aye," he answered. McRory seemed to have confidence to spare, but William's own was beginning to flag, especially after such an impersonal greeting.

After all that had passed between them, she was still calling him "MacKenzie"?

William shrugged in irritation. "*He* hasn't recently suffered a twenty-foot fall and a sleepless night." Or for that matter, a potentially broken heart.

Her lips quirked up, but she still didn't look at him. "Do you regret not g-getting a good night's sleep?"

His eyes settled on the smooth curve of her cheek. The sun had been fierce today, and he could see a slight redness to her skin.

Or perhaps it was a remnant of last night's activities.

"No. I would not trade my night for another." He shook his head, knowing it was true. He might be an idiot, but he was a happy idiot, for however long her attentions were focused on him. "And as for the caber, there's more to the toss than brute strength," he reminded her.

"Yes, as you've said." A serene smile claimed her face, but it held a bit of the devil in it. "And I've a notion you know how to aim your stick."

She stared straight ahead, as though they hadn't been tangled skin to skin last night and as though they weren't carrying on a conversation filled with enough innuendo to sink a ship. He looked hungrily at her, wanting only to take her by the arm and drag her into some private corner, his own upcoming toss with the caber be damned.

McRory was taking his time, nodding to the crowd as though born for the stage, and damned if he didn't shoot Pen a confident, toothless smile. She waved back in a manner that made William's fists clench. Then, with an inhuman growl, the butcher ran a few steps and launched the caber in the air. The entire crowd watched with collective, indrawn breaths as the log arced, end over end, landing with a thump William could feel in his bones.

It was the farthest throw yet.

The crowd's approval was loud enough to wake the dead. McRory took a dramatic bow, his kilt riding dangerously high. William looked at Pen, wondering if she was impressed.

But in that moment, he realized she hadn't been watching McRory.

She was looking at *him*.

And the look of hunger on her face mirrored his own.

As his own name was called, William took his place on the line, his head buzzing with what that look may have meant. The crowd quieted. He looked down at the caber that had been laid for him. It looked nearly the length of a mile. He bent and hefted the log onto his shoulder, testing its balance, and then adjusted his grip in slow increments until the tip seemed to nearly touch the sky. And then, with no heart for the sort of theatrics favored by the butcher, and with Pen's face occupying his thoughts, he took the running steps required for the right momentum. At the last moment, he gave a mighty heave and imagined he was tossing McRory's mangy, melodramatic carcass high in the sky.

The caber soared. End over end, in a perfect arc. The crowd shaded their eyes, some doubting, others hoping.

It landed a few inches short of McRory's.

But unlike McRory's toss, William's caber landed perfectly straight.

The crowd erupted in a roar of applause and whistles, rushing the field and lifting him high. Amid the congratulatory cheers and backslaps, William twisted, trying to catch a glimpse of Pen, knowing her approval, alone, was what he sought.

He caught her eye, just as they carried him toward Main Street, and it was only later he'd realized her notebook had been nowhere in sight.

Pen walked among the crowd, sipping a pint of ale purchased from a local vendor. She didn't need to write down any more notes to remember this day. Indeed, she was beginning to suspect she might be missing some key parts of life to always have her nose buried in a notebook. It had taken coming to Moraig to show her that.

And she only wanted this evening to last forever.

Night had fallen, but in the flickering torchlight, bodies were spinning and feet were flying. The scent of wood smoke filled her nose, easily overcoming the press of heated bodies, and the din of camaraderie echoed in her ears. The day may have been devoted to the games, but it seemed the evening belonged to a less competitive sort of chaos. Music flowed steadily, along with the ale, and there was a well-inebriated edge to the crowd. Nearly everyone was dancing, caught up in the toe-tapping rhythm coming from the pipers on the stage. She was content to merely watch, mesmerized by the pounding tempo and the acrobatics on display, knowing he would come.

Suddenly MacKenzie was there before her, emerging like a Highland dream. He bowed in his plaid, which no longer seemed ridiculous. Perhaps it was because every able-bodied male in sight was wearing a kilt of some sort today.

Or perhaps it was because she now knew the contours of the body that lurked beneath.

"Miss Tolbertson," he said in a formal voice, making her clap a hand over her mouth to hold back a giggle. He took the near-empty cup from her hand and unceremoniously tossed it over one shoulder. "I believe you promised me a dance."

"I did." She gestured to the people spinning and leaping around them. "B-but I am not familiar with these steps."

"'Tis naught but a jig." His grin deepened, and in the torchlight his teeth flashed like a promise. Whatever hesitancy he'd initially felt around her seemed to have been banished by the night they had shared, and she was glad for it. "Why, wee babes can do it. In their sleep."

She laughed, unable to take her eyes from his face. "While the jig looks lovely, I had a different sort of dance in mind." She did not want to waste a moment if hours were all they had left. Already she was achingly aware of the fact that the coach left at eight o'clock sharp tomorrow morning and that her bag was already packed, waiting on the bureau of her room at the Blue Gander. She had not been able to kiss him a proper good-bye this morning.

Which meant, of course, she needed to correct the oversight tonight.

But bless his sometimes thick head, he did not seem to get her meaning. "If you prefer to wait for a fling, you have only to say the word. 'Tis a favorite of the crowd, you ken. The pipers will probably play one next."

She flushed, knowing she wanted a different sort of fling.

But unfortunately, a fling was all it could be. In the few days she had known him, it was evident how much he loved Moraig. His family. She respected his devotion for those things, even as she wished desperately to grab some of it and keep it for herself.

But it would not be fair for her to expect—or want—more.

She had seen the way the town had rallied around him when he'd won the caber toss.

He belonged here, with them, and they needed him more than she did.

"MacKenzie." She said his name like the prayer it was and stepped closer, until her dress brushed against his plaid. She was admittedly a little sore—though not so sore those parts of her weren't declaring their intentions for more. Heat bloomed along her skin, remembering how he had touched her last night. "The dance I want involves privacy," she whispered.

There was a beat of silence, filled only by the heart-pounding rhythm of the pipers.

And then he inclined his head, and his hand was reaching out to grab hers. "Your wish is my command, lass."

And then he pulled her into the night.

Chapter Eight

"MacKenzie," Pen hissed. She fumbled for his hand, and as his palm met hers, she tightened her fingers over it. Given the steep, downward descent of the path, she could only guess they were aiming for Loch Moraig again. "I d-do not wish to see the crodh mara tonight."

And the dance she'd had in mind would benefit from a bed.

"Trust me, lass," was all he said, giving her hand an encouraging squeeze.

So she followed him, her hand clasped tight in his, turning herself over to whatever he had in mind. He'd not failed her yet in that regard. Indeed, he'd proven himself capable of delivering some astonishing surprises. Perhaps there was even a symmetry here, a return to the place where this connection between them had started.

Or had that place been the posting house, when she'd first seen him standing at attention, sweat dripping down his face?

At last the trees thinned out, letting the moon shine down. They emerged at the edge of the loch, and Pen drew in a sharp breath at the sheer beauty of it. The water glittered in the moonlight, ripples of light that seemed to grow and spread like a living thing. She could hear the bellow of cattle, but it seemed a distant sound, perhaps a half mile or more away.

As her eyes adjusted to the change in light, she realized they were not standing in the cow field, as she'd expected, but at the base of some ancient ruins. The tumbled stone walls were around chest height, and whatever roof had once graced the structure had long since fallen to the ravages of time and climate.

"Are these the ruins of the original c-castle?" she asked in wonder, reaching out a tentative hand to touch the stones. They were cool beneath her fingers and slick with moss.

"No, this was once a Roman outpost." He tugged her hand, pulling her deeper into the maze of tumbled rocks. "My father is a scholar of Caledonian history, and we've dug for artifacts here on several occasions."

"I thought your f-father was the Earl of Kilmartie," Pen said in confusion.

He dropped her hand and moved away in the moonlight. "He was a scholar first. I suppose, in a way, he's a scholar still. I studied history myself at Cambridge. Visitors interested in history will find a rich heritage in these hills. I thought you might wish to write about it."

"Oh," Pen said, her head spinning at yet another facet to the man who was William MacKenzie. Heir. Benefactor. Son of a scholar.

She exhaled, wondering which part she was coming to love.

All of them, she suspected.

"Is this where the artifacts in my room came from?" she said, remembering the beautiful pieces on display in her room at the Gander.

"Aye. I dug those myself."

She bit her lip, knowing what she was about to say sounded selfish. "This is lovely, t-truly." She squinted, trying to see what he was doing in the meager light. "But I've only a few hours left. Surely you didn't bring me down here to d-dig for artifacts."

His low chuckle warmed her ears. "No lass." Dimly, she could see him unbolting his plaid, and her pulse kicked up a healthy notch. "I know you've a bit of the adventurer in you. I've a mind to give you an authentic Highland experience, aye?"

"Aye," she whispered, her heart now pounding in full agreement.

He unwound the plaid from his body, and she watched him with a hunger that made her question whether she was meant to be a spinster after all. Surely a woman content to spend her life in the company of newspapers should feel a bit more embarrassment watching a man undress under moonlight. It seemed endless, that plaid, and yet far too short, because all too soon he was standing only in his shirt tails, his strong, muscled legs braced apart.

Pen swallowed her nervousness. "Verra nice," she told him, purposefully rolling her tongue into the burr she heard on every street corner.

He chuckled and then pulled his shirt over his head in a smooth, efficient motion.

She sucked in a breath. She'd seen him last night, of course. Traced her hands over those bulging arms and calves, pressed kisses to places that even now made her blush at the thought. But that had been at close range, in a bed, safe and artificial. She'd not had a sense of the entirety of him. Standing nude in the moonlight, surrounded by the trees and rocks, the sound of the nearby water lapping in her ears, he was a far more potent assault to her senses.

The son of an earl had no business looking so...so...so *perfect*.

Had she once questioned his status as the most handsome man in a room? How naïve she had been, to judge a man's attractiveness solely on the basis of his smile. Or for that matter, to insist on a room. The architecture of his muscles seemed to perfectly complement the night. Her gaze swung lower, to the part of his anatomy that had caused her that slight bit of pain last night.

There was even beauty to be found there, if one only had an opportunity to look.

He was giving her that opportunity, and more, it seemed.

He spread his plaid on the grassy earth. Lowering himself onto it, he patted the ground for her to follow. She dropped to her knees and then whooped out loud as his arm snaked around her and she was flipped onto her back.

"Close your eyes," his graveled voice whispered in her ear.

She obeyed, keeping them closed even when the tug of fabric and the rush of cool night air on her skin told her he was undressing her as well.

The plaid-covered grass felt soft beneath her back, as soft as any bed, and it was no hardship to lie still while his fingers brushed against her newly exposed skin. In the imposed darkness, her other senses felt heightened. Her skin prickled in anticipation, gooseflesh being the natural response to both the cool night air and MacKenzie's touch. In her ears, the night sounds reigned—insects, water, and the distant lowing of cattle all combining in a delicate symphony.

She felt alive, aware of her surroundings and the potential in her own body in a way she never had before. He had given her these gifts, pulled her from her world of books and pencils and notebooks, and shown her that to know life, one had to experience it, not only write about it.

She felt the warmth of his mouth on her shoulder, a kiss pressed to skin. "Now open them," he commanded, "and look straight above."

She did. And was promptly lost in the beauty of the sky.

It was stunning. Midnight blue, with just a faint rim of light on the horizon. Stars spilled across the canvas of sky, so brilliant as to hurt her eyes. She blinked, wondering how this could be the same sky she'd seen all week.

"It looks d-different," she gasped.

She felt his lips trail down her bare arm and shivered into the feel of him. "The walls of the ruins block the moonlight as it reflects off the surface of the loch," he explained. "So the effect of the stars is intensified."

"Oh," she breathed and then nearly whimpered as his mouth met hers, warm and insistent.

Had she thought the night perfect before? *Now* it was perfect, his kiss so deep as to make her feel as though they were breathing the same air. He pulled her closer, and she welcomed the heat of his body, pressed fully against her front, the cooler air at her back.

It would hurt to say good-bye to this man tomorrow.

But for now, at least they had tonight.

He was already dreading the end, but William tried hard to focus on the opportunity now in his hands. She was here tonight, lying in his arms and bathed in starlight.

They could worry about the leaving later.

He kissed her as though there was no tomorrow. Pressed his mouth to secret, fragrant places, until she writhed beneath him and cried out his name. She still called him *MacKenzie*, though, rather than *William*. He was determined to eventually change her mind.

She tasted like home—sweet, earthy ale from the Gander and salt-slick summer days—and her skin carried the faint scent of lemons from the soap she used. He licked at the indentation of her collarbone, nipped at the delicate skin of her neck, as though she were a cake laid out to assuage his appetite. His fingers swept across the curls that guarded her secrets, and the moisture there told him how much she wanted this.

Wanted him.

He slid a finger inside her warmth and lowered his head against her neck, breathing in deeply. Bloody hell. "No sponge this time?" he nearly groaned in frustration.

She shook her head. "I had thought to p-put it in when we went back to the room." He could feel her body quake as his finger swirled inside her. "You surprised me." She gasped in pleasure. "P-perhaps it won't matter?"

He released the breath he hadn't known he was holding. Having Pen naked in his arms was like holding a loaded gun. And Christ above, he wanted to make love to her, here, on the banks of Loch Moraig, where she wouldn't soon forget her visit. Forget *him*.

If they made a child tonight, it would be a way to keep her, he was sure of it.

But could he live with himself, knowing he had trapped her in such a way?

He was not sure he had the strength to do what he was about to promise, but he didn't see another way. "I won't spill my seed inside you," he told her.

She nodded, clearly trusting him.

He only hoped he trusted himself.

He slid inside her, and the feel of her body and the slight sound she made there in the back of her throat—the same sound, in fact, she had made during their first kiss—nearly made him break that promise.

He stilled. Let his body settle and adjust to the bright white pleasure of simply being inside her. And then he began to move. She moved with him, her head tipped back, and tonight he could see she kept her eyes open, as though not wanting to miss a moment.

He placed his hands on either side of her face and stared down into those beautiful, wide-open eyes, holding her close as he moved inside her. He murmured to her in Gaelic and comforted himself with the knowledge she need never know he'd just told her how much he loved her. All too soon she was shuddering beneath him, coming apart in his arms, and he knew he had but seconds to earn the trust she had so willingly placed in his hands.

He pulled from her, finishing the last few strokes himself.

And then he collapsed, pulling her so tightly against his chest he was probably bound to crush her. But she didn't protest, only burrowed deeper with a melting sigh of contentment.

He pulled the edges of the plaid around them, shielding her against the night's cool air. Her breathing slowed, and at the sign of her recovery, he kissed her fair shoulder, knowing the moment of reckoning was here.

"I love you, lass."

She stiffened. "You d-don't mean that." Her voice sounded muffled against his chest. "We hardly know each other."

"I do, Pen. I would marry you tonight if you would but have me. And we could, too. The blacksmith is just beyond Main Street."

He could feel her start to shake, but was it with emotion or regret?

"MacKenzie," she said, her voice small and uncertain.

"William," he nearly growled.

"I've a j-job in London. An assignment to complete." She pulled away from him, her hands pressed flat against his chest. "You've known that from the start."

"I ken you've a job to do. I can respect that." And if his plans for Moraig were to be realized, he needed her to return. He swallowed, an idea swimming drunkenly in his mind. He could not imagine living anywhere but Moraig, but neither could he imagine living without her. "I could come with you to London. I would make you a good husband, Pen."

"I d-don't need a husband," she protested, sitting up now and fishing about in the dark for her clothes. Her voice sounded on the verge of panic.

He shook his head. "I dinna say you needed a husband, lass." He hesitated, knowing it came down to this. "The question is, do you want one?"

In the darkness, her face seemed very pale and unsure. "I...I d-don't know." She stood up and clasped her gown against her front, but it couldn't hide the way she was trembling. "I would make a *t-terrible* c-countess." She cringed. "My stammer means I would b-be judged. *You* would be judged. You d-deserve someone normal."

"I disagree. You would make a brilliant countess." He shook his head. "And if I'd wanted someone normal, I wouldn't have kissed you to start."

"I kissed you first," she said miserably.

"Not tonight." He tried to smile. "I don't want normal, Pen. I want brilliant. And you are that and more." He was ready to kiss her again, to prove to her they belonged together.

But now she was throwing a hand to one side, gesturing toward the loch. "C-can't you see? This isn't about *me*, MacKenzie. I c-can't see you living in London. You might as well try to put your water cattle in the Serpentine. It would kill you. Kill your spirit, the thing that makes you who you are. You belong *here*. In Scotland. Surrounded by p-people you know and love." She shook her head, as if it was all too obvious. "You belong in Moraig."

His heart felt heavier than the damn caber. "I belong with you, lass."

She jerked her gown over her head. "You don't understand." She drew a deep breath and then faced him. "I don't want you to c-come to London."

Her eyes glittered through the darkness. He felt as though she could see right through him but yet couldn't see a thing in front of her. He was suddenly very aware of his own nudity. It hadn't mattered when she'd been staring at him in want, but now that she was rejecting him, he felt a burning need to cover himself.

He spent an inordinate amount of time arranging his plaid. In his heart, he agreed with her—to a point. As the heir to the Earl of Kilmartie, his rightful place was here, in Moraig. Moreover, he didn't want to leave the Highlands. He loved this country, had never been more miserable than the four years he'd spent at Cambridge.

But he'd meant it when he said he loved her. Following her to London was a sacrifice he was willing to make if it meant keeping her.

And if the city was so terrible, why was she so determined to return?

"Will you at least think on my offer?" he asked gruffly.

She did not answer.

He pulled the plaid around him and then gained his feet and belted it into place. He had one more thing to say to her, and he hoped she was listening. "I ken you're a good reporter, Pen. I can see it in the way you work, the questions you ask. I'm not asking you to give that up. I would come to you, wherever you decided to live. But living a life of loneliness is no life at all." He hesitated. "I know, because it's the life I've led until now."

In the darkness, he could hear her swallow.

"I won't press you, if the thought of me coming to London is so distasteful. 'Tis your choice, and if you go, know you are always welcome to return, whenever you want. But you don't need to be independent to prove yourself to other people, or to me. I ken how brave you are. But perhaps it's sometimes braver to risk your heart, aye?"

She stood motionless. Wordless.

And he knew then that he'd lost her. She was going back to London. Without him.

And there wasn't a damn thing he could do to stop her.

The London Times, Tuesday, August 22, 1843

AN IDYLLIC SETTING IN
MORAIG, SCOTLAND

by P. Tolbertson

It is rare that a holiday changes your life.

Most people travel for a bit of adventure or perhaps a well-deserved rest. Others travel to visit a location of historical significance and spend their time prowling for artifacts or knowledge. But it is uncommon to find a place that has all these things and moreover leaves you transformed by the experience.

Moraig, Scotland, is that place, and more.

Londoners seeking an escape from the swelter of summer can find no more perfect idyll and should set their sights on this charming little town posthaste. Visitors are greeted by men draped in ancient plaids, their Highland heritage on full and proud display. Refreshing breezes off the nearby Atlantic coast and well-furbished rooms at the local inn tempt you to spend the entire holiday in a state of relaxation. At night, Moraig's residents enjoy a bit of revelry, and the town boasts a dozen varieties of fine Scottish whisky. Try the local ale at the Blue Gander's public room, and be sure to ask for Miss Sally, who will serve you a wink along with your pint. History lovers will appreciate Kilmartie Castle and the ruins along the shores of Loch Moraig. Keep an eye out for the crodh mara, fairy creatures who emerge from the loch under moonlight— they might very well steal your desire to return home.

And should you find your heart captured by the loveliness of the town or perhaps one of its residents, do not despair. The local blacksmith can marry you, if you've a notion. And if you are unsure of your heart, remember…

There is always next year.

CHAPTER NINE

"You're an idiot."

William rolled his eyes, given that this was at least the third time this week he'd been told something of the sort, most recently by his brother, James. The fact that the latest claim came from McRory did little to soothe his fraying temper.

"Aye." He glared at the butcher. "You'll not find an argument from me there. But we need every able-bodied man between the ages of fifteen and fifty to stand in their plaid and greet the tourists. Today is your turn, and I dinna particularly care if you object or not."

McRory scowled. "Ye daft nubbin, this isn't about the plaid. You are an idiot to have let Miss Tolbertson go."

A growl loosened in William's chest to have the conversation circle predictably around to Pen. He understood he was an idiot in that vein as well, and the entire town took every opportunity to remind him. "I dinna *let* her do anything. She decided her own way."

"Well, you've been nothing but unpleasant since she left two months ago, and you're as liable to scare the bloody tourists off as welcome them."

Oh, for Christ's sake. Was no one on *his* side? Pen had made quite an impression during her short week here, and her newspaper article and the ensuing flood of tourists had lifted her legend to staggering new heights. He had no doubt that if she deigned to visit them again, she'd be greeted with the sort of enthusiasm more appropriately reserved for the queen.

On account of this—or perhaps in spite of it—the general consensus was that he was not only a bloody idiot, but a lovestruck fool as well.

But short of following Pen to London—an idea to which she had clearly conveyed her displeasure—he had no idea how to fix his foul temper.

"If she'd taken a shine to me," McRory went on, scratching his beard, "you could bet *I* would not have let her flit off to London. Why did you not go after her? I would not have pegged you for a coward."

"I'm not a coward." William's collar suddenly felt overtight despite the day's perfectly pleasant temperature. "I'm a gentleman."

But he wasn't a gentleman, not really. Because a primitive part of him agreed with McRory, and he was getting bloody well tired of arguing with his conscience.

The butcher shrugged. "I see very little difference from where I stand."

William pointed across the street, where a rowdy, masculine crowd had begun to gather outside the Gander to get their first glimpse at the day's tourists. "Then go stand over there."

"And miss my turn with the coach?" McRory grinned, showing the gap between his front teeth. "Why, the future Mrs. McRory might be on it, and today I mean for my lap to be the first she sees."

"Oh, for heaven's sake." William stared down the road, trying to think of anything but the butcher's lap. At least the weather had started to cool off. The October sun was bright but unthreatening, which was a good thing, given that he was draped in wool nearly every day now. Never his brightest idea, the bloody plaid had been mentioned in Pen's newspaper article, and now every visitor from London expected to be greeted by a Highlander's bare knees.

William only prayed the curious visitors would trickle off come winter. He wasn't looking forward to a stiff Highland breeze then.

Down the road, a cloud of dust rose up, signaling the imminent arrival of Mr. Jeffers. That was odd. He checked his pocket watch. It was close to three o'clock.

Was Jeffers...*early*?

McRory peered at the approaching cloud of dust and then, with an eagerness that didn't bode well for the day's crop of tourists, spit in his hand and slicked it over his hair. "Well, with you moping about like a kicked dog, I suppose it means the ladies will be mine today." He grinned. "Good thing I've lap enough for all of them."

Mr. Jeffers roared up in his usual haphazard manner. But rather than unloading tourists, he began to unload boxes. *Lots* of boxes, and a machine that looked suspiciously like an oven, but with wheels and gears. "What is all this?" William demanded. "Where are the visitors?"

"Only one visitor today," Jeffers answered, heaving a large crate down from the top of the coach and placing it in McRory's waiting hands. "But she's an important one. She might need a hand, if you're of a mind to help her." He paused in his exertions long enough to wink down at them. "I hear this one especially likes a man in plaid."

McRory dropped his crate and surged ahead, and William let him go. After all, the future Mrs. McRory might be on board. William had no heart for it, anyway.

Because every new coach reminded him of the day Pen had roared into town.

And every day that passed without her reminded him of all he had lost.

A rustle of skirts met his ears. "Welcome to Moraig," McRory crowed.

"Thank you, k-kind sir."

Surely he was hearing things, his imagination playing tricks on him again. But those sleights of memory usually came at night, when he was alone and vulnerable and wanting. His eyes whipped to level, and he nearly choked on his surprise.

Pen stood beside the coach, as beautiful as she was in his dreams.

But this time she was real. She *must* be, because she was wearing far too many clothes.

William knocked a very bemused McRory out of the way and picked up the woman his heart refused to forget, swinging her around until she was whooping and wheezing all at once.

"MacKenzie," she laughed. "P-put me down a moment, so I can speak."

He did but made sure she knew of his appreciation for the sight of her by sliding her slowly down the front of his plaid. Her gasp told him she'd recognized his enthusiasm.

"Oh my," she said. "That *is* a lovely g-greeting."

He took a step back, suddenly aware of their audience. Worse, his own uncertainties regarding the nature of her return began to crowd in. Perhaps she wasn't here to see him. Perhaps she'd come to see Caroline, who was about to start her lying-in.

Or perhaps the *Times* had sent her on another investigative matter.

The truth was he simply didn't know why she was here, and it might have nothing to do with him. And so he waited for her say to something, hope humming in his throat.

She tilted her head. "You look t-tired, MacKenzie."

"Aye. I've not been sleeping well," he admitted, but it was a fact he couldn't see remedying tonight. She was here. He'd just held her in his arms.

Sleep was the furthest thing from his mind.

He looked at the boxes Jeffers was still unloading. They made a veritable tower in the dusty street. His heart leaped with hope at the thought she might stay longer than a week. "How long will you stay this time?" he dared to ask, knowing he would gladly take whatever it was and try not to worry about her next leaving.

"That d-depends."

He blinked down at her.

Her smile was serene, but it held a hint of mischief as well. "Do you think Moraig might b-benefit from having its own newspaper?"

It took a moment for her words to find a foothold, and even then they felt slippery in his brain. "I dinna understand."

"I had thought to start one." She raised a pale brow. "Counter the t-town's rumor mill with facts, for a change."

"You mean…You are moving here? To Moraig?"

She nodded. "I've brought a small printing press. Nothing close to a real press, mind you, but it will serve to produce a small local paper."

"You are coming to start a newspaper?" he repeated, his head buzzing like a hive of hornets. She nodded again, and his heart strained toward her. "But…*why?*"

Her blue eyes shone with good humor. "Are you sure you g-graduated summa some-aught from Cambridge, MacKenzie?"

Behind him, he could hear McRory snigger.

She tilted her head. "Why d-do you think, you thick-witted Highlander? I've missed you. And you *did* tell me I could return, whenever I wanted."

He looked confused, poor thing. Absolutely brained by it all.

This time, though, she couldn't blame him for his confusion.

It had been two months since he had seen her, two months where he'd been largely oblivious to the degree of misery that had consumed her. All he knew was that she'd left, returned to London alone. He had no way of knowing she'd done so not only because of the commitment she'd made to the paper, but because the moments she'd spent in his arms hadn't seemed quite real.

But most of all, she had left because as tempted as she'd been by his offer, she couldn't see herself being so selfish as to take MacKenzie away from the townspeople who needed him.

But it *had* been real. Perhaps the most real thing she'd ever had.

Far more real than London, fairy creatures included. The city's streets had seemed sour after the wholesomeness of Moraig's dusty thoroughfares, and the smog-choked skies smothered the life out of every star that dared to shine. Nor could she bear to write to him and explain these things, when her words—the only thing she might conceivably count as a talent—seemed to dry up on the paper.

She'd felt hollow inside. Trapped. Lost.

Until Caroline—bless her sisterly heart—had written of MacKenzie's own misery, suggesting that perhaps she had left a piece of her heart behind in Moraig.

It may have taken her two months to understand the emotion, but there was no hesitancy now. He'd given her the time and space she had asked for—things she now knew had come at his own personal cost. A generous man was William MacKenzie. So concerned with the welfare of others he would sacrifice himself.

How could she not have seen it from the start?

She traced the hollows beneath his eyes, vowing to make them disappear.

"I love you, MacKenzie." She smiled, knowing she would never again falter over those words because they came from her heart, not her throat.

"You dinna ken how much I have wanted to hear you say that." A slow, spreading smile claimed his face. "Well. *Most* of that." His voice lowered. "If you are going to be here awhile, do you think you might at least call me *William*, lass?"

She choked on her laugh. "P-probably not. A man would have to marry a woman to earn that privilege I think."

He stepped toward her. "Are you proposing to me, Miss Tolbertson?"

Anticipation bunched in her chest. She lifted her chin to look up the impossible length of him. "Are you accepting my p-proposal, MacKenzie?"

Brown eyes glittered down at her. "You don't do anything the traditional way, do you?"

She only smiled. Serenely, she hoped.

He dropped to his bare knees in the dust of Main Street, and suddenly she found herself in the astonishing position of looking down on him. McRory and Jeffers began to slap each other on the back, as though their happiness belonged to everyone. From across the street, she could hear excited whoops and whistles, sounds that echoed the cacophony in her own heart.

"Careful of those bare knees, MacKenzie!" came a disembodied voice.

"Have a care, you dinna want to show her your arse!"

He ignored the taunts of the townspeople and looked up at her, his eyes warm on her skin. "Will you marry me, Pen?"

"Yes," she said and then giggled at how simple the word was to say, after all this time. "*William*."

And then she was in his arms, knocking them both off balance. They tumbled into the dirt and grit, not even caring about their audience. Because the cheer that erupted behind her told her they approved of whatever it was they were seeing beneath MacKenzie's plaid.

And then her mouth found his, and she was sliding into a kiss that felt like coming home. "I missed you," she murmured against his lips. "More than I'd thought p-possible."

"You don't have to miss me anymore. It doesn't matter where we live, as long as we are together, aye?"

"Aye," she sighed in pleasure and kissed him again.

Keep reading for a special sneak peek at

DIARY OF AN ACCIDENTAL WALLFLOWER,

the first book in Jennifer McQuiston's
anticipated new series!

*Pretty and popular, Miss Clare Westmore knows exactly
what (or rather, who) she wants: the next Duke of
Harrington. But when she twists her ankle on the eve
of the Season's most touted event, Clare is left standing
in the wallflower line watching her best friend
dance away with her duke.*

*Dr. Daniel Merial is tempted to deliver more than a
diagnosis to London's most unlikely wallflower, but he doesn't
have time for distractions, even one so delectable. Besides,
she's clearly got her sights on more promising prey.
So why can't he stop thinking about her?*

*All Clare wants to do is return to the dance floor. But as her
former friends try to knock her permanently out of place,
she realizes with horror she is falling for her doctor instead of
her duke. When her ankle finally heals and she faces her old
life again, will she throw herself back into the game?*

*Or will her time in the wallflower line have given her a
glimpse of who she was really meant to be?*

COMING FEBRUARY 2015

A Sneak Peek at

DIARY OF AN ACCIDENTAL WALLFLOWER

CHAPTER ONE

Miss Clare Westmore wasn't the only young woman to fall head over heels for Mr. Charles Alban, the newly named heir to the Duke of Harrington.

Though, she was probably the only one to fall quite so literally.

He appeared out of nowhere, broad shouldered and perfect, trotting his horse down one of the winding paths near the Serpentine. His timing was dreadful. For one, it was three o'clock on a Friday afternoon, hardly a fashionable hour for anyone to be in Hyde Park. For another, she'd come down to the water with her siblings in tow, and the ducks and geese they'd come to feed were already rushing toward them like a great, screeching mob.

Her sister, Lucy, poked an elbow into her ribs. "Isn't that your duke?"

Clare's heart galloped well into her throat as the sound of hoofbeats grew closer. What was Mr. Alban *doing* here? Riders tended to contain themselves to Rotten Row, not this inauspicious path near the water. If he saw her now, it would be an unmitigated disaster. She was wearing last Season's walking habit—fashionable enough for the ducks, but scarcely the modish image she wished to project to the man who could well be her future husband. Worst of all, she was with Lucy, who brushed her hair approximately once a week, and Geoffrey, who ought to have been finishing his first year at Eton but who had been expelled just last week for something more than the usual youthful hijinks.

Clare froze in the center of the milling mass of birds, trying to decide if it would be wiser to lift her skirts and run or step behind the cover of a nearby rhododendron bush. One of the geese took advantage of her indecision, and its beak jabbed at her calf through layers of silk and cotton. Before she knew what was happening—or could even gather her wits into something resembling a plan—her thin-soled slipper twisted out from under her, and she pitched over onto the ground with an unladylike *oomph*. She lay there, momentarily stunned.

Well then. The rhododendron it was.

She tucked her head and rolled into the shadow of the bush, ignoring low-hanging branches that reached out for her. The ducks, being intelligent fowl, followed along. They seized the crumpled bag of bread still clutched in her hand and began gulping down its contents. The geese—being, of course, quite the opposite of ducks—shrieked in protest and flapped their wings, stirring up eddies of down and dust.

Clare tucked deeper into the protection of the bush, straining to hear over the avian onslaught. Had she been seen? She didn't think so. Then again, her instincts had also told her no one of importance would be on this path in Hyde Park at three o'clock on a Friday afternoon, and look how well those thoughts had served.

"Oh, what fun!" Lucy laughed, every bit as loud as the geese. "Are you playing the damsel in distress?"

"Perhaps she is studying the mating habits of waterfowl," quipped Geoffrey, whose mind always seemed to be on the mating habits of *something* these days. He tossed a forelock full of blond hair out of his eyes as he offered her a hand, but Clare shook her head. She didn't trust her brother a wit. At thirteen years old and five and a half feet, he was as tall as some grown men, but he retained an adolescent streak of mischief as wide as the Serpentine itself.

He was as likely to toss her into Alban's path as help her escape.

Lucy cocked her head. Wisps of tangled blond hair rimmed her face like dandelion fluff and made her appear far younger than her seventeen years, though her tall frame and evident curves left no doubt that she was old enough to show more care with her appearance. "Shall I call Mr. Alban over to request his assistance then?" she asked, none too innocently.

"Shhhh," Clare hissed. Because the only thing worse than meeting the future Duke of Harrington while dressed in last year's walking habit was meeting him while wallowing in the dirt. Oh, but she should never have worn such inappropriate shoes to go walking in Hyde Park. Then again, such hindsight came close to philosophical brilliance when offered up from the unforgiving ground.

She held her breath until the sound of hoofbeats began to recede into the distance. Dimly, she realized something hurt. In fact, something hurt dreadfully. But she couldn't quite put her finger on the source when her mind was spinning in the more pertinent directions.

"Why are you hiding from Mr. Alban?" Lucy asked pointedly.

"I am not hiding." Clare struggled to a sitting position and blew a wayward brown curl from her eyes. "I am...er... feeding the ducks."

Geoffrey laughed. "Unless I am mistaken, the ducks have just fed themselves, and that pair over there had a jolly good tup while the rest of them were tussling over the scraps. You should have invited your duke to join us."

"He's not yet a duke," Clare corrected crossly. Much less *her* duke.

But oh, how she wanted him to be.

"Pity to let him go by without saying anything. You could have shown him your overhanded throw, the one you use for Cook's oldest biscuits." Geoffrey pantomimed a great, arching throw out into the lake. "*That* would impress him, I'm sure."

The horror of such a scene—and such a brother—made Clare's heart thump in her chest. To be fair, feeding the ducks was something of a family tradition, a ritual born during a time when she hadn't cared whether she was wearing last year's frock. These days, with their house locked in a cold, stilted silence and their parents nearly estranged, they retreated here almost every day. And she *could* throw Cook's biscuits farther than either Lucy or Geoffrey, who took after their father in both coloring and clumsiness. It was almost as if they had been cut from a different bolt of cloth, coarse wool to Clare's smooth velvet.

But these were not facts one ought to share with a future duke—particularly when that future duke was the gentleman you hoped would offer a proposal tonight. No, better to wait and greet Mr. Alban properly this evening at Lady Austerley's annual ball, when Lucy and Geoffrey were stashed safely at home and she would be dressed in tulle and diamonds.

"I don't understand." Lucy stretched out her hand, and this time Clare took it. "Why wouldn't you wish to greet him? He came to call yesterday, after all, and I was given the impression you liked him very much."

Clare pulled herself to standing and winced as a fresh bolt of pain snatched the breath from her lungs. "How do you know about that?" she panted. "I didn't tell anyone." In fact, she'd cajoled their butler, Wilson, to silence. It was imperative word of the visit be kept from their mother, who—if last Season's experience with potential suitors was any indication—would have immediately launched a campaign to put Waterloo to shame.

"I know because I spied on you from the tree outside the picture window." Lucy shrugged. "And didn't you say that he asked you to dance last week?"

"Yes," Clare agreed between gritted teeth. Mr. Alban *had* asked her to dance last week, a breathless waltz that had sent the room spinning and held all eyes upon them. It was the third waltz they had shared since the start of the Season— though not all on the same night, more's the pity. But the glory of that dance paled in comparison to the dread exacted by Lucy's confession.

Had her sister really hung apelike from a limb and leered at the man through the window? Except…hadn't Alban sat with his back to the window?

She breathed a sigh of relief. Yes, she was almost sure of it.

He'd spent the entire quarter hour with his gaze firmly anchored on her face, their conversation easy. But despite the levity of their exchange, he'd seemed cautious, as though he were hovering on the edge of some question that never materialized but that she fervently wished he'd just *hurry up and ask*.

Given his unswerving focus, there was no way he would have seen her clumsy heathen of a sister swinging through the branches, though she shuddered to think that Lucy could have easily lost her balance and come crashing through the window in a shower of broken glass and curse words. But thankfully, nothing of the sort had happened. No awkward siblings had intruded on the flushed pleasure of the moment. Her mother had remained oblivious, distracted by her increasing irritation with their father and her shopping on Bond Street.

And to Clare's mind, Mr. Alban had all but declared his intentions out loud.

Tonight, she thought fiercely. Tonight would be the night when he asked for more than just a dance. And that was why it was very important for her to tread carefully, until he was so irrevocably smitten she could risk the introduction of her family.

"I *do* admire him," she admitted, her mind returning reluctantly to the present. "I just do not want him to see me looking like…" Clare glanced down at her grass-stained skirts and picked at a twig that had become lodged in the fabric. "Well, like this."

Lucy frowned. "I scarcely think his admiration should be swayed by a little dirt."

"And you didn't look like that before you dove behind that bush," Geoffrey pointed out. "Stunning bit of acrobatics, though. You ought to apply to the circus, sis."

"I didn't dive behind the bush." Clare battled an exasperated sigh. She couldn't expect either of them to understand. Lucy still flitted through life not caring if her hair was falling down. Such obliviousness was sure to give her trouble when she came out next year. Clare herself couldn't remember a time when she hadn't been acutely aware of every hair in its place, every laugh carefully cultivated.

And Geoffrey was…well…*Geoffrey*.

Loud, male, and far too crude for polite company.

As a child, the pronounced differences between herself and her siblings had often made her wonder whether perhaps she had been a foundling, discovered in a basket on the front steps of her parents' Mayfair home. She loved her siblings, but who wouldn't sometimes squirm in embarrassment over such a family?

And what young woman wouldn't dream of a dashing duke, destined to take her away from it all and install her within the walls of his country estate?

Clare took a step, but as her toe connected with the ground, the pain in her right ankle punched through the annoyance of her brother's banter. "Oh," she breathed. And then, as she tried another step, "*Ow*! I…I must have twisted my ankle when I fell."

"I still say you dove," Geoffrey said with a smirk.

Lucy looked down with a frown. "Why didn't you say something?" she scolded. "Can you put any weight on it at all?"

"I didn't realize at first." Indeed, Clare's mind had been too much on the threat of her looming social ruin to consider what damage had been done to her person. "And I am sure I can walk on it. Just give me a moment to catch my breath."

She somehow made her way to a nearby bench, ducks and geese scattering like ninepins. By the time she sat down, she was gasping in pain and battling tears. As she slid off her dainty silk slipper, all three of them peered down at her stocking-encased foot with collective indrawn breaths. Geoffrey loosened an impressed whistle. "Good God, sis. That thing is swelling faster than a prick at a bawdy show."

"Geoffrey!" Clare's ears stung in embarrassment, though she had to imagine it was an apt description for the swollen contours of her foot. "This is not Eton, we are not your friends, and that will be *quite* enough."

"Don't you have Lady Austerley's ball tonight?" Lucy asked, her blue eyes sympathetic. "I can't imagine you can attend like this. In fact, I feel quite sure we ought to carry you home and call for the doctor, straightaway."

But Clare's mind was already tilting in a far different direction. This evening's ball hadn't even crossed her mind when she had been thinking of the pain, but now she glared down at her disloyal ankle. *No, no, no.* This could not be happening. Not when she was convinced Mr. Alban would seek her out for more than just a single dance tonight.

It didn't hurt so much when she was sitting.

Surely it would be better in an hour or so.

"Of course I can go." Clare struggled to slip her shoe back on, determined to let neither doubts nor bodily deficiency dissuade her. "Just help me home, and don't tell Mother," she added, "and everything will be fine."

CHAPTER TWO

"You belong in bed, not in a ballroom."

Dr. Daniel Merial chased this medical opinion with his most impressive glower and prayed his patient would see reason. He'd been summoned to No. 36 Berkeley Square by a furtive note, delivered to the morgue at St. Bartholomew's Hospital. He'd come immediately, no matter that he'd been forced to abandon a body lying half dissected on the theater table. The deceased was of unusual height and abnormal bone density, and a cataloging of the body's physical findings would have lent itself well to a paper on the subject.

But it was an opportunity now lost.

The physician who'd taken over the case had seemed far more interested in helping the students position the corpse into grotesque, suggestive poses than locating a pencil to record his findings. It irked Daniel to turn a perfectly interesting cadaver over to a fool like that, but St. Bart's was full of pompous young doctors whose positions had been secured by wealthy fathers willing to contribute to a new hospital wing, rather than any clear demonstration of intelligence. Unlike them, *he* needed to supplement his meager instructor's salary by serving as a personal physician to the wealthy and cantankerous, at the beck and call of London's elite.

Though this patient, in particular, was proving a very troublesome case.

Lady Austerley's lips thinned—if indeed, an aging dowager countess's lip could thin any more than nature already commanded. "Cancelling my annual ball is not an option, Dr. Merial. It is seven o'clock already. Half of London will be summoning their coaches, and the other half will be lamenting their lack of an invitation." She rubbed her gnarled hands together. "Now, surely you have some more of that marvelous medication. It helped so much the last time you gave it to me."

Daniel sighed, suspecting this irksome venture could be explained by little more than an old lady's lonely pride. It had not escaped his notice that he was one of Lady Austerley's most frequent—indeed, one of her only—visitors. Her husband was long dead, and their forty-year union had not been blessed with children. The cousin who had inherited her husband's title never came to call. She'd outlived her friends, and now she seemed determined to outlive her heart.

"The belladonna extract is a temporary fix, at best," he warned, "and may well do more damage to your heart in the long term. What you *need* is rest, and plenty of it."

"But I *am* resting." Lady Austerley offered him a smile, one that showed her false ivory teeth in all their preternatural glory. "You see, I am lying down on the bed while my maid curls my hair." As if offering testimony to this nonsensical thought, the pink-cheeked maid—who'd been casting him dream-filled glances since his arrival—pulled the curling tongs from her mistress's thinning gray hair with an audible hiss.

"And I promise not to dance," the countess continued, "if you would but leave a draught or two, enough to get me through this evening."

Daniel was sorely tempted to leave her laudanum instead, but he wasn't sure he had the heart to deceive her into sleep. Lady Austerley could be difficult, but she had also been his first substantial client in London. Her remarkable and unexpected patronage had opened the doors of his fledgling practice, and he was only now beginning to attract the occasional notice of other well-connected clients.

But that didn't mean she actually *listened* to him.

His client might be lying down in bed, but she was also already dressed for her ball, swaddled in a gown of gold brocade that at turns threatened to asphyxiate and dazzle. The room should have smelled of camphor, but instead it smelled of French perfume and the faint, acrid scent of burning hair. "I told you weeks ago you were making yourself ill, Lady Austerley." He ran a frustrated hand through his hair. "You ought to have cancelled the event then. Instead, you've exhausted yourself with preparations."

"You did tell me my remaining time fell on the side of months, rather than years, did you not?" At his nod, she shrugged her thin shoulders—unapologetically, to Daniel's mind. "I am determined to make my last days memorable and give them all something they won't soon forget. What was that bit of Latin you quoted for me?"

Her expectant pause made him want to fidget. "*Quam bene vivas referre, non quam diu,*" he admitted reluctantly.

It is how well you live that matters, not how long.

He'd offered her the phrase soon after it became clear her condition was carrying her surely and steadily toward the grave. But he'd meant to encourage her to reflect on the life she had led. He'd certainly not intended it to be a dictum for how she should go on.

Her frown shifted to a wrinkled smile. "There, you see?" she beamed, quite pleased with herself. "I am just following my doctor's orders."

"Lady Austerley, you must know you are shortening the time you have left by the very choices you make now. You could easily suffer another fainting spell tonight, even with the medication," he warned. "You were fortunate your maid was attending you during your bath this afternoon when the latest one struck, or you might have drowned. This is the second attack you've experienced this week, is it not?"

The dowager countess nodded innocently.

"My lady is perhaps forgetting several spells," the maid piped up. "By my count, it is the fourth such episode since Monday."

Lady Austerley turned her gimlet glare on the younger woman. "Am I to count higher mathematics among your skills as my lady's maid now? I cannot believe you bothered our beleaguered doctor with that note. I imagine it had as much to do with *you* wishing to see him again as any need for me to. You've been mooning over him for months."

The poor maid blushed, but not before her eyes darted tellingly in Daniel's direction. "I was thinking only of your health, my lady."

"Hrmmph." Lady Austerley lifted the quizzing glass she always kept around her neck, and he felt the sting of the older woman's visual dissection. "Not that I blame you," she added, a wrinkled smile playing about her lips. "He's a stunning specimen, with all that thick, dark hair and those soulful brown eyes. Makes an old woman's heart flutter, even one who's heart is just barely ticking along. Truth be told, he puts these new London bucks to shame."

Daniel raised a brow, determined to circle this conversation away from the issue of whether or not he was considered attractive to the female species and back around to the medical issue at hand. "Lady Austerley," he said sternly.

But she was not yet through. She lowered her lens and struggled to a sitting position as the maid plumped her pillow. "It's his heart that makes him different, though. Heart of gold, to come rushing to an old lady's aid like this. These young men today can't be bothered to look further than their phaetons for entertainment."

Daniel fought the urge to roll his eyes.

"I would have you come to the ball tonight and put my theory to the test, Dr. Merial." Lady Austerley lifted her quizzing glass again. "Yes, yes, my personal physician in attendance. That would be just the thing to show them all."

Daniel breathed in through his nose. Show them what, precisely? Her loss of sanity? He was tempted to dismiss her nattering as the beginnings of dementia. But alas, he knew there was nothing at all wrong with Lady Austerley's head. She was as lucid as a lark.

He might have stood a better chance at changing her mind if she wasn't.

"It sounds as though your attacks are increasing in frequency, as I predicted they would. Your heart is failing. You should be confined to your bed, if not to ward off these periods of syncope, to at least ensure when they occur you do not risk falling and causing more serious injury." He took in the dowager countess's impossibly straight back. "And didn't I advise against wearing a corset? You cannot afford to restrict your breathing further."

Lady Austerley waved a fist, the ropey veins crisscrossing the backs of her hands like twisted paths to truth. "I cannot have a ball without a corset, and as I've already said, I refuse to entertain the notion of cancelling the event. I must carry on, at least until tonight is behind me. Which is why I need you there, in case I suffer another spell."

"I cannot prevent these attacks," he informed her gravely. "I can only advise you on what you must do to reduce their frequency."

"Perhaps you cannot prevent them, but I will feel better knowing you are there." She tossed a bemused look at her maid, who was still stargazing in Daniel's direction. "And if I should be so unfortunate as to feel off balance again, surely if you are already present, we can manage another episode with far less drama than this afternoon's little spell has entailed."

The maid blushed further and tucked her head.

Daniel hesitated. He enjoyed spending time with the dowager countess, but he already had plans for this evening, plans that involved patients who actually *listened* to him— namely, the unfinished cadaver he'd left lying prone on the theater table. If he agreed to this farce of an idea, he would need to slip back to his rooms now to bathe and dress instead of returning to the morgue. He'd also planned another phase of his experiment for later this evening, testing varying doses of a promising new compound called *chloroform* with the anesthetic regulator he was developing. Losing valuable hours at a ball was not high on his list of priorities.

Although, if he were brutally honest, tonight's event might benefit him in the long run. He was very afraid Lady Austerley might not live to see Christmas. He would regret the eventual loss of that income, though not as much as he would regret the loss of her sometimes prickly friendship. Tonight would be an opportunity for introductions to future clients, if nothing else.

The countess leaned back against her mountain of plush pillows, and her hand crept out to grab his own. Her frail touch was a shock. He could feel her thready pulse, beating faintly through her bones, hinting at coming trouble. "I would ask this of you, Dr. Merial. As a favor to a scared old lady whose heart needs to last through at least one more ball."

Daniel swallowed his misgivings. How could he say no to such a request?

She had no family to speak of, no remaining close friends. She was lonely and ailing, and he'd been unable to refuse the dowager countess anything since their first chance meeting, when she'd fainted dead away in St. Paul's Cathedral and he'd been the only one with enough sense to come to her aid. He squeezed her hand. "If it would ease your mind."

"Excellent." Lady Austerley smiled. "I'll have an invitation penned for you, posthaste."

CHAPTER THREE

Clare's ankle wasn't better in an hour or so.

Neither had it improved by the time the coach was brought around to the front door, nor by the time she stepped into Lady Austerley's vaulted foyer. If anything, it was worse, sporting whimsical new shades of red and purple and stealing her breath with every step.

"Do try to keep up, dear." Her mother frowned over her shoulder, the red feather on her headdress bobbing with discontent. "I declare, you dawdle more like your father every day."

Clare gritted her teeth. She could not admit to her mother the real reason for her hesitation, or else risk being whisked home to bed. And any comparisons to Father were to be avoided if her mother was to remain in an ebullient mood this evening. She hobbled faster, her mismatched shoes clunking ominously on the marble tile.

Step, thump. Step, thump.

Her mother didn't seem to notice, but Clare's cheeks heated at the disparate sounds. She ought to be grateful Lucy was possessed of overlarge feet and, moreover, had been willing to donate an old shoe to the nearly lost cause of getting her foot into something approximating a slipper. At least she hadn't needed to resort to wearing *Geoffrey's* shoe.

But gratitude was not foremost on Clare's mind as her mother gave their name to the footman. She lifted her chin, knowing that aside from the travesty of her mismatched shoes, she had never looked better. Her maid had taken hours with her hair, and her new green gown was an absolute wonder, clinging to her shoulders with what appeared to be nothing more than hasty prayer. But though the gown's voluminous skirts hid her feet from public view, they could not change the fact her ankle still felt like a sausage shoved in a too-tight casing.

She looked out on the glittering swirl of London's most beautiful people, her stomach twitching in anticipation. The ballroom was awash with colors and scents, by now familiar after the triumph of her first Season. She knew what to expect, whom to greet, and whom to cut. And somewhere in the crowd Mr. Alban waited, a proposal surely simmering on his tongue.

Almost immediately she was set upon by her usual pack of friends, and her mother drifted off. "Where have you *been?*" Lady Sophie's fan snapped open and shut in agitation, though her eyes sparkled with mischief.

"Mr. Alban arrived nearly a half hour ago," Rose supplied helpfully.

Clare fit a careful half smile to her face as she greeted her friends. Lady Sophie Durston always stood out like a dark hothouse flower amidst the crowd, though this evening she stood out more because of her vivid pink gown. Miss Rose Evans was a classic English beauty, blond and blue-eyed. Tonight she was dressed in virginal white—though Sophie had snidely confided to Clare just last week that perhaps Rose should avoid that color, and not only because it was a miserable complement to the girl's too-pale complexion.

They were the young women all the men watched and the less fortunate girls envied. Together they had captured the hearts and imaginations of half the eligible men in the room. But since the start of this Season, Clare had been interested in only one of those hearts, and her friends knew it all too well.

She risked a veiled peek in Mr. Alban's direction. He was speaking with Sophie's father, a pompous windbag of an earl who had recently helped secure Parliament's new ban on public meetings. Intended to hobble supporters of the growing Chartist movement, the news had been splashed across all the papers and bandied about polite Society in hushed, worried tones. She briefly wondered which side of the debate Alban claimed, though it was something she could never ask during the space of a waltz.

But as the overhead chandelier caught the white flash of his teeth, those distracting thoughts fell away. Oh, but he looked resplendent tonight in a dark jacket and emerald waistcoat, his chestnut hair gleaming. She could almost see him looking just so across a morning breakfast table, polished to a shine by her careful attentions, the *Times* spread out amicably between them. "Has Mr. Alban asked anyone to dance?" she asked, turning away from the heart-stopping sight of him so she could not be accused of mooning overlong.

"Not just yet," Rose piped up from Sophie's elbow, where she almost always hovered like a pale, blond shadow.

"He's been speaking with Father since he arrived," Sophie confirmed, her voice a low purr. "Business over pleasure, you know."

Clare was relieved to hear he had not been busy with other girls' dance cards, though she wasn't worried. Mr. Alban had been remarkably persistent in asking her to dance the first waltz each evening. She harbored no doubts that this evening would go the same way.

As the musicians began to take their seats behind the screen of potted greenery that had been erected to hide them from view, a young man approached their group with the sort of enthusiasm usually displayed by unruly puppies—or, barring that, their eight-year-old owners.

"Good evening, Miss Westmore."

Clare sighed, knowing she must acknowledge him. "Good evening, Mr. Meeks."

He beamed at her, though she'd gifted him with the barest of greetings. "I was honored last week when you said you would grant me the first dance this evening."

Clare gripped her dance card. Had she really done something so rash? He was a perfectly unthreatening specimen of a young man, but he was also one of the gentlemen Mother had encouraged far too enthusiastically last year. Still, Clare was predisposed to be kind. He meant well, even if he didn't make her heart stir with anything other sympathy.

And she liked to think she *would* have honored her agreement to dance with the young man, had things been different. But the conversation with Meeks had occurred one week and one turned ankle ago. She could scarcely be expected to honor such a promise given her current circumstances.

"I am afraid you must have misunderstood." She shook her head, knowing her ankle was unlikely to last more than a dance or two. "I am otherwise engaged."

He deflated before her eyes. "Oh. I see." His feet shuffled as he turned to Sophie and Rose, a nervous sheen on his high forehead. "Perhaps, then, if either of you are free?"

Sophie shook her head in mock regret. "I am afraid you are far too tardy in asking, Mr. Meeks. Our cards are already full." She pointed her fan toward a line of restless young ladies sitting against the far wall of the ballroom. "You might aim your sights over there. I feel sure someone in the wallflower line will still have a few open spots remaining for a gentleman of your punctuality."

Mr. Meeks's cheeks flared with color as Rose tittered behind a gloved hand. As he turned away and began to trudge toward the wallflower line, Clare sighed. "Honestly, Sophie, was it necessary to be so cruel? He's done naught to earn our ire."

"Oh, don't look so glum," Sophie chided. She flicked her fan open and fluttered it lazily below her green eyes. "Truly, the occasional set-down is the best thing all around for him. Have you forgotten about that debacle last year, when he had the gall to think you might consider his proposal?" The air rang with her light laughter. "It isn't as though he should harbor hopes for anything beyond the occasional dance where *we* are concerned."

Clare held her tongue. It was true she had set her sights higher than a proposal from Meeks, but that did not mean she thought it was all right to snub him. There were some in the crowd who thought she *should* have accepted his proposal, her mother among them. After all, Mr. Meeks had an annual income of two thousand pounds and would one day be a viscount, the same title as her own father. There was potential there, to be sure.

But Sophie had decided, based on some unfathomable criteria only she knew, that Mr. Meeks was not within their sphere.

In contrast, though he was only the heir presumptive to a dukedom, Mr. Alban had been immediately welcomed into Sophie's circle. Of course, he was handsome as sin, something Mr. Meeks had no hope of claiming. Furthermore, the elderly Duke of Harrington was clearly consumptive, and, rumor had it, none too interested in females, so Alban was as good as the heir apparent in many eyes.

Still, it frightened Clare sometimes to see how unpredictable the tide of public opinion could be. Next year Lucy would be out among this harsh crowd, and in a few short years Geoffrey would also be navigating this same social gauntlet. She didn't like to think that her siblings—embarrassing though they may be—might be similarly sized up and dismissed.

So tonight she offered her friends nothing more questionable than an agreeable nod. Because being included in Sophie's gilded circle was far better than being shoved outside it, and she'd worked too hard to get here to ruin it tonight in a fit of misplaced kindness.

As the opening strains of the first set of the evening rang out, Sophie's lips curved upward. "Not that I would ever question your desire to wait for a better offer than was afforded by Mr. Meeks, but you've just arrived."

"Yes," Rose added, suspicion adding a half octave to her voice. "What was that nonsense about being otherwise engaged? You can't have a single name on your dance card yet."

"I…I might sit out the first set." At their looks of horror, Clare tried to smile, though she suspected it came out more as a grimace. "I'm a little fatigued this evening. I might prefer to save my strength to dance with Mr. Alban."

"You do look a trifle pale." Sophie's hand reached out to gently squeeze Clare's arm. "Heavens, what are we thinking, chattering away like magpies when you look close to swooning? You need to sit down and rest." She inclined her head toward the row of chairs she had earlier pointed out to Meeks. "There's a prime seat, just there. Now, which dance were you hoping for from Alban? Maybe I can help hurry him along."

Clare contemplated the vicious throbbing of her foot. The wallflower line was the furthest thing from a refuge, but it was also becoming increasingly obvious her ankle would be unlikely to tolerate more than a turn or two around the dance floor. "I think I should be recovered by the first waltz of the evening," she replied, eyeing the empty chair as if it might have teeth. "If you speak with Mr. Alban, you might offer him such a hint."

Sophie's smile deepened as her own partner arrived to collect her for the first dance. "Of course," she tossed over one shoulder, already gliding toward the dance floor. "You know I would do anything for a friend."

Death was rarely—if ever—a laughing matter.

Pity, that.

Daniel supposed it took a man with a sense of humor to prefer to stay with a rotting corpse and a room full of eager young medical students rather than attend a ball. Still, he had promised Lady Austerley he would come tonight, and a promise made to a lonely, ailing countess was one you oughtn't break, unless the death you contemplated was your own.

Newly scrubbed and dressed in his best jacket, he greeted the dowager countess with a clinical eye, noting the pale fragility of her skin and the way her hands shook slightly through her gloves. Though the overhead chandeliers blazed with light, her pupils were dilated, providing some reassuring evidence the atropine he had given her earlier was still working.

"You look well tonight," Daniel lied, lifting her hand to his lips. "I see you have chosen to partially heed my advice and greet your guests while seated. Still, I would be negligent in my duties if I did not advise you that lying down would be the preferred course of action."

Lady Austerley's lips twitched. "If I were forty years younger I would blush to hear such a thing from a handsome gentleman, Dr. Merial." She squeezed his hand. "Now. You may have come out of medical necessity, but I very much hope you will enjoy yourself this evening, because I have no intention of embarrassing myself with anything so gauche as a fainting spell. Perhaps you would do me the honor of a dance later?"

Daniel smiled down at the older woman. "Of course," he agreed, though they both knew the countess would not be dancing tonight, and probably never again.

As he moved on, searching for a space along the wall that would permit him a good view of his patient, he recognized a peer he had recently treated, a man whose various health woes he could catalog down to a resting heart rate. "Good evening, Lord Hastings," Daniel nodded.

The gentleman stiffened and turned away. For a moment Daniel was perplexed. Had he been incorrect in his address? Somehow rude in his delivery? But then he overheard another person greet the man, and he knew he'd had the right of it.

Ah, so *that's* how it was going to be.

When he was summoned to their homes to deal with a medical complaint, he was greeted with the sort of desperation reserved of a savior. But let him step among their ranks with an invitation in his pocket, and such niceties were lost.

The ladies in attendance, however, were a decidedly different story. Several among the painted and perfumed crowd ducked their heads behind their fans, then came back for a second, surreptitious look. Daniel had been in London only six months now, but already he understood why *these* women—women who had husbands and wealth and boredom to burn—looked at him with hooded eyes, fluttering fans, and undisguised interest. It was not comfort they were seeking.

He was young. He was handsome. He was *here*.

And those were apparently the only criteria to be considered.

He'd sidestepped their bold offers until now, but perhaps he'd been going about this all wrong, courting the male heads of these households in his bid to win more clients. He didn't doubt he could leave tonight with several new female patrons, if he applied a modicum of charm.

Or—given the way several smiled invitingly—an eager new bed partner or two.

Though he was tempted to test this theory by smiling back at them, Daniel aimed for the east side of the ballroom instead, where the crowd opened up and a row of chairs lined the wall. As he threaded his way there, he realized that Lady Austerley had been right to be concerned she might suffer one of her increasingly frequent dizzy spells tonight. The heat from the overhead chandeliers was stifling, and the mingling scents of beeswax and floral perfume made his own stomach feel off-kilter.

Worse, however, was the noise. All around him nonsensical conversations swirled like eddies of dust caught in the wind. This blond-haired chit felt another's gown was a simply *awful* shade of puce. That one shuddered to hear such a third-rate cellist sawing on the strings. One graying matron loudly bemoaned the fact the heads had been left on the prawns, no doubt to mock those guests possessed of more delicate sensibilities.

Though on the surface everyone was smiling, the undercurrent of female malcontent caught him by surprise. He could not help but feel there was something unhealthy about smiling to one's hostess in one moment and disparaging her in the next. Hadn't they come here tonight to honor the dowager countess, who, in her day, had been a widely admired figure? Though he knew she preferred to keep the details of her diagnosis private, anyone with a pair of functioning eyes could see the signs of the countess's declining health and realize this was Lady Austerley's last annual ball.

He wedged himself against a wall and scowled out at the crowd. Though it was difficult to credit the emotion, given that he was at a bloody ball, boredom began to creep in.

Lady Austerley, bless her bones, was holding her own from her chair near the entrance to the ballroom, and looked to require no immediate assistance. He had no desire to dance, and refused to consider the horrors of puce or prawns, one way or the other.

Indeed, he had no desire to sample any of the diversions on offer here tonight.

Step, thump. Step, thump.

A sound cut through the drivel of small talk, and Daniel turned his head to search for its source. In the midst of such glitter and polish, that incongruous sound seemed his greatest hope to encounter something more thought-provoking tonight than third-rate cellists. He suffered an almost irrational disappointment to see nothing more interesting than a young lady approaching. A brunette, slim, and exceptionally attractive young lady, to be sure, but really no different than any of the other tittering flora and fauna on display tonight.

Step, thump. Step, thump.

Well, except for *that*.

His clinical skills flared to life. A few inches over five feet, but probably less than seven stone. She was within a year or two of twenty, though on which side she fell was little more than an educated guess. He had always been an ardent student of the human form, favoring symmetry over chaos, and his eye was drawn as much to the finely wrought curve of this girl's bones as the rich brown hair piled on top of her head. Her neck alone was an anatomist's dream, long and elegant, drawing the eye to the prominent line of her shoulders.

She flashed a half smile at someone who passed and he caught a glimpse of not-quite-perfect teeth, though the minor misalignment of her left cuspid did little to lessen the impression of general loveliness. If anything, it heightened his sense that she was real, rather than a porcelain doll waiting to be broken.

His eyes lingered a moment on the stark prominence of her clavicles, there above her neckline. She could stand to gain a few pounds, he supposed.

Then again, couldn't they all?

Step, thump. Step, thump.

That part was deucedly odd. She didn't appear outwardly lame, though her shuffling gait lacked the smooth refinement he expected in young ladies of the fashionable set. She settled herself into an empty seat along the wall and carefully arranged her skirts, but not before he caught the edge of one hideously ugly shoe peeking out from beneath the hem of her gown.

Now that she was sitting still, her symptoms told him a far different story than the one delivered by her fixed half smile. Her gloved hands sat on her lap, the picture of feminine innocence, but as he watched, they knotted and unknotted in the shimmering green of her skirts, seeking traction against some unseen force. Her forehead was creased in concentration, and beads of perspiration had formed above her upper lip.

He well knew the signs. Either the chit was constipated or in severe pain.

He was betting on the latter.

And just like that, the evening's entertainment shifted toward something far more promising than Lady Austerley's staunch refusal to faint.

Or even, God help him, the corpse.

ABOUT THE AUTHOR

A veterinarian and infectious disease researcher by training, **JENNIFER MCQUISTON** has always preferred reading romance to scientific textbooks. She resides in Atlanta, Georgia, with her husband, their two girls, and an odd assortment of pets, including the pony she promised her children if Mommy ever got a book deal. Jennifer can be reached via her website at www.jenmcquiston.com or followed on Twitter @jenmcqwrites.

Discover great authors, exclusive offers, and more at hc.com.

Give in to your impulses . . .
Read on for a sneak peek at seven brand-new
e-book original tales of romance
from Avon Impulse.
Available now wherever e-books are sold.

HOLDING HOLLY
A Love and Football Novella
By Julie Brannagh

IT'S A WONDERFUL FIREMAN
A Bachelor Firemen Novella
By Jennifer Bernard

ONCE UPON A HIGHLAND CHRISTMAS
By Lecia Cornwall

RUNNING HOT
A Bad Boys Undercover Novella
By HelenKay Dimon

SINFUL REWARDS 1
A Billionaires and Bikers Novella
By Cynthia Sax

RETURN TO CLAN SINCLAIR
A Clan Sinclair Novella
By Karen Ranney

RETURN OF THE BAD GIRL
By Codi Gary

An Excerpt from

HOLDING HOLLY
A Love and Football Novella
by Julie Brannagh

Holly Reynolds has a secret. Make that two.
The first involves upholding her grandmother's
hobby of answering Dear Santa letters from
dozens of local schoolchildren. The second . . .
well, he just came strolling in the door.

Derrick has never met a woman he wanted to
bring home to meet his family, mostly because
he keeps picking the wrong ones—until he
runs into sweet, shy Holly Reynolds. Different
from anyone he's ever known, Derrick realizes
she might just be everything he needs.

"**D**o you need anything else right now?"

"I'm good," he said. "Then again, there's something I forgot."

"What do you need? Maybe I can help."

He moved closer to her, and she tipped her head back to look up at him. He reached out to cup one of her cheeks in his big hand. "I had a great time tonight. Thanks for having pizza with me."

"I had a nice time too. Th-thank you for inviting me," she stammered. There was so much more she'd like to say, but she was tongue-tied again. He was moving closer to her, and he reached out to put his drinking glass down on the counter.

"Maybe we could try this again when we're not in the middle of a snowstorm," he said. "I'd like a second date."

She started nodding like one of those bobbleheads, and forced herself to stop before he thought she was even more of a dork.

"Yes. I . . . Yes, I would too. I . . . that would be fun."

He took another half-step toward her. She did her best to pull in a breath.

"Normally, I would have kissed you good night at your front door, but getting us inside before we froze to death seemed like the best thing to do right then," he said.

"Oh, yes. Absolutely. I—"

He reached out, slid his arms around her waist, and pulled her close. "I don't want to disrespect your grandma's wishes," he softly said. "She said I needed to treat you like a lady."

Holly almost let out a groan. She loved Grandma, but they needed to have a little chat later. "Sorry," she whispered.

He grinned at her. "I promise I'll behave myself, unless you don't want me to." She couldn't help it; she laughed. "Plus," he continued, "she said you have to be up very early in the morning to go to work, so we'll have to say good night."

Maybe she didn't need sleep. One thing's for sure, she had no interest in stepping away from him right now. He surrounded her, and she wanted to stay in his arms. Her heart was beating double-time, the blood was effervescent in her veins, and she summoned the nerve to move a little closer to him as she let out a happy sigh.

He kissed her cheek, and laid his scratchier one against hers. A few seconds later, she slid her arms around his neck too. "Good night, sweet Holly. Thanks for saving me from the snowstorm."

She had to laugh a little. "I think you saved *me*."

"We'll figure out who saved who later," he said. She felt his deep voice vibrating through her. She wished he'd kiss her again. Maybe she should kiss *him*.

He must have read her mind. He took her face in both of his hands. "Don't tell your grandma," he whispered. His breath was warm on her cheek.

"Tell her what?"

"I'm going to kiss you."

Her head was bobbing around as she frantically nodded yes. She probably looked ridiculous, but he didn't seem to care. Her eyelids fluttered closed as his mouth touched hers, sweet and soft. It wasn't a long kiss, but she knew she'd never forget it. She felt the zing at his tender touch from the top of her head to her toes.

"A little more?" he asked.

"Oh, yes."

His arms wrapped around her again, and he slowly traced her lips with his tongue. It slid into her mouth. He tasted like the peppermints Noel Pizza kept in a jar on the front counter. They explored each other for a while as quietly as possible, but maybe not quietly enough.

"Holly, honey," her grandma called out from the family room. Holly was *absolutely* going to have a conversation with Grandma when Derrick was out of earshot, and she stifled a groan. All they were doing was a little kissing. He rested one big hand on her butt, which she enjoyed. "Would you please bring me some salad?"

Derrick let out a snort. "I'll get it for you, Miss Ruth," he said loudly enough for her grandma to hear.

"She's onto us," Holly said softly.

"Damn right." He grinned at her. "I'll see you tomorrow morning." His voice dropped. "We're *definitely* kissing on the second date."

"I'll look forward to that." She tried to pull in a breath. Her head was spinning. She couldn't have stopped smiling if her life depended on it. "Are you sure you don't want to stay in my room instead? You need a good night's sleep. Don't you have to go to practice?"

"I'm sure your room is very comfortable, but I'll be fine out here. Sweet dreams," he said.

She felt him kiss the top of her head as he held her. She took a deep breath of his scent: clean skin, a whiff of expensive cologne, and freshly pressed clothes. "You, too," she whispered. She reached up to kiss his cheek. "Good night."

An Excerpt from

IT'S A WONDERFUL FIREMAN
A Bachelor Firemen Novella
by Jennifer Bernard

Hard-edged fireman Dean Mulligan has never
been a big fan of Christmas. Twinkly lights and
sparkly tinsel can't brighten the memories of too
many years spent in ramshackle foster homes.
When he's trapped in the burning wreckage of
a holiday store, a Christmas angel arrives to
open his eyes. But is it too late? This Christmas,
it'll take an angel, a determined woman in love,
and the entire Bachelor Firemen crew to make
him believe . . . it is indeed a wonderful life.

He'd fallen. Memory returned like water seeping into a basement. He'd been on the roof, and then he'd fallen through, and now he was . . . here. His PASS device was sounding in a high-decibel shriek, and its strobe light flashed, giving him quick, garish glimpses of his surroundings.

Mulligan looked around cautiously. The collapse must have put out much of the fire, because he saw only a few remnants of flames flickering listlessly on the far end of the space. Every surface was blackened and charred except for one corner, in which he spotted blurry flashes of gold and red and green.

He squinted and blinked his stinging eyes, trying to get them to focus. Finally the glimpse of gold formed itself into a display of dangling ball-shaped ornaments. He gawked at them. What were those things made from? How had they managed to survive the fire? He sought out the red and squinted at it through his face mask. A Santa suit, that's what it was, with great, blackened holes in the sleeves. It was propped on a rocking chair, which looked quite scorched. Mulligan wondered if a mannequin or something had been wearing the suit. If so, it was long gone. Next to the chair stood half of a plastic Christmas tree. One side had melted into black goo, while the other side looked pretty good.

Where am I? He formed the words with his mouth, though no sound came out. And it came back to him. Under the Mistletoe. He'd been about to die inside a Christmas store. But he hadn't. So far.

He tried to sit up, but something was pinning him down. Taking careful inventory, he realized that he lay on his left side, his tank pressing uncomfortably against his back, his left arm immobilized beneath him. What was on top of him? He craned his neck, feeling his face mask press against his chest. A tree. A freaking Christmas tree. Fully decorated and only slightly charred. It was enormous, at least ten feet high, its trunk a good foot in diameter. At its tip, an angel in a gold pleated skirt dangled precariously, as if she wanted to leap to the floor but couldn't summon the nerve. Steel brackets hung from the tree's trunk; it must have been mounted somewhere, maybe on a balcony or something. A few twisted ironwork bars confirmed that theory.

How the hell had a Christmas tree survived the inferno in here? It was wood! Granted, it was still a live tree, and its trunk and needles held plenty of sap. And fires were always unpredictable. The one thing you could be sure of was that they'd surprise you. Maybe the balcony had been protected somehow.

He moved his body, trying to shift the tree, but it was extremely heavy and he was pinned so flat he had no leverage. He spotted his radio a few feet away. It must have been knocked out of his pouch. Underneath the horrible, insistent whine of his PASS device, he heard the murmuring chatter of communication on the radio. If he could get a finger on it, he could hit his emergency trigger and switch to Channel 6, the May Day channel. His left arm was useless, but he could try with his right. But when he moved it, pain ripped through his shoulder.

Hell. Well, he could at least shut off the freaking PASS device. If a rapid intervention team made it in here, he'd yell for them. But no way could he stand listening to that sound for the next whatever-amount-of-time it took. Gritting his teeth against the agony, he reached for the device at the front of his turnout, then hit the button. The strobe light stopped and sudden silence descended, though his ears still rang. While he was at it, he checked the gauge that indicated how much air he had left in his tank. Ten minutes. He must have been in here for some time, sucking up air, since it was a thirty-minute tank.

A croak issued from his throat. "I'm in hell. No surprise." *Water.* He needed water.

"I can't give you any water," a bright female voice said. For some reason, he had the impression that the angel on the tip of the Christmas tree had spoken. So he answered her back.

"Of course you can't. Because I'm in hell. They don't exactly hand out water bottles in hell."

"Who said you're in hell?"

Even though he watched the angel's lips closely, he didn't see them move. So it must not be her speaking. Besides, the voice seemed to be coming from behind him. "I figured it out all by myself."

Amazingly, he had no more trouble with his throat. Maybe he wasn't really speaking aloud. Maybe he was having this bizarre conversation with his own imagination. That theory was confirmed when a girl's shapely calves stepped into his field of vision. She wore red silk stockings the exact color of holly berries. She wore nothing else on her feet, which had a very familiar shape.

Lizzie.

His gaze traveled upward, along the swell of her calves. The stockings stopped just above her knees, where they were fastened by a red velvet bow. "Christmas stockings," he murmured.

"I told you."

"All right. I was wrong. Maybe it's heaven after all. Come here." He wanted to hold her close. His heart wanted to burst with joy that she was here with him, that he wasn't alone. That he wasn't going to die without seeing Lizzie again.

"I can't. There's a tree on top of you," she said in a teasing voice. "Either that, or you're very happy to see me."

"Oh, you noticed that? You can move it, can't you? Either you're an angel and have magical powers, or you're real and you can push it off me."

She laughed. A real Lizzie laugh, starting as a giggle and swooping up the register until it became a whoop. "Do you really think an angel would dress like this?"

"Hmm, good point. What are you wearing besides those stockings? I can't even see. At least step closer so I can see."

"Fine." A blur of holly red, and then she perched on the pile of beams and concrete that blocked the east end of his world. In addition to the red stockings, she wore a red velvet teddy and a green peaked hat, which sat at an angle on her flowing dark hair. Talk about a "hot elf" look.

"Whoa. How'd you do that?"

"You did it."

"I did it?" How could he do it? He was incapacitated. Couldn't even move a finger. Well, maybe he could move a finger. He gave it a shot, wiggling the fingers on both hands. At least he wasn't paralyzed.

But he did seem to be mentally unstable. "I'm hallucinating, aren't I?"

"Bingo."

An Excerpt from

ONCE UPON A HIGHLAND CHRISTMAS

by Lecia Cornwall

Lady Alanna McNabb is bound by duty
to her family, who insist she must marry a
gentleman of wealth and title. When she meets
the man of her dreams, she knows it's much
too late, but her heart is no longer hers.

Laird Iain MacGillivray is on his way to propose
to another woman when he discovers Alanna
half-frozen in the snow and barely alive. She isn't
his to love, yet she's everything he's ever wanted.

As Christmas comes closer, the snow
thickens, and the magic grows stronger.
Alanna and Iain must choose between
desire and duty, love and obligation.

Alanna McNabb woke with a terrible headache. In fact, every inch of her body ached. She could smell peat smoke, and dampness, and hear wind. She remembered the storm and opened her eyes. She was in a small dark room, a hut, she realized, a shieling, perhaps, or was it one of the crofter's cottages at Glenlorne? Was she home, among the people who knew her, loved her? She looked around, trying to decide where exactly she was, whose home she was in. The roof beams above her head were blackened with age and soot, and a thick stoneware jug dangled from a nail hammered into the beam as a hook. But that offered no clues at all—it was the same in every Highland cott. She turned her head a little, knowing there would be a hearth, and—

A few feet from her, a man crouched by the fire.

A very big, very naked man.

She stared at his back, which was broad and smooth. She took note of well-muscled arms as he poked the fire. She followed the bumps of his spine down to a pair of dimples just above his round white buttocks.

Her throat dried. She tried to sit up, but pain shot through her body, and the room wavered before her eyes. Her leg was on fire, pure agony. She let out a soft cry.

He half turned at the sound and glanced over his shoulder, and she had a quick impression of a high cheekbone lit by the firelight, and a gleaming eye that instantly widened with surprise. He dropped the poker and fell on his backside with a grunt.

"You're awake!" he cried. She stared at him sprawled on the hearthstones, and he gasped again and cupped his hands over his— She shut her eyes tight, as he grabbed the nearest thing at hand to cover himself—a corner of the plaid— but she yanked it back, holding tight. He instantly let go and reached for the closest garment dangling from the line above him, which turned out to be her red cloak. He wrapped it awkwardly around his waist, trying to rise to his feet at the same time. He stood above her in his makeshift kilt, holding it in place with a white knuckled grip, his face almost as red as the wool. She kept her eyes on his face and pulled her own blanket tight around her throat.

"I see you're awake," he said, staring at her, his voice an octave lower now. "How do you feel?"

How *did* she feel? She assessed her injuries, tried to remember the details of how she came to be here, wherever here might be. She recalled being lost in a storm, and falling. There'd been blood on her glove. She frowned. After that she didn't remember anything at all.

She shifted carefully, and the room dissolved. She saw stars, and black spots, and excruciating pain streaked through her body, radiating from her knee. She gasped, panted, stiffened against it.

"Don't move," he said, holding out a hand, fingers splayed, though he didn't touch her. He grinned, a sudden flash of white teeth, the firelight bright in his eyes. "I found you out in the snow. I feared . . . well, it doesn't matter now. Your knee is injured, cut, and probably sprained, but it isn't broken," he said in a rush. He grinned again, as if that was all very good news, and dropped to one knee beside her. "You've got some color back."

He reached out and touched her cheek with the back of his hand, a gentle enough caress, but she flinched away and gasped at the pain that caused. He dropped his hand at once, looked apologetic. "I mean no harm, lass—I was just checking that you're warm, but not too warm. Or too cold . . ." He was babbling, and he broke off, gave her a wan smile, and stood up again, holding onto her cloak, taking a step back away from her. Was he blushing, or was it the light of the fire on his skin? She tried not to stare at the breadth of his naked chest, or the naked legs that showed beneath the trailing edge of the cloak.

She gingerly reached down under the covers and found her knee was bound up in a bandage of some sort. He turned away, flushing again, and she realized the plaid had slipped down. She was as naked as he was. She gasped, drew the blanket tight to her chin, and stared at him. She looked up and saw that her clothes were hanging on a line above the fireplace—all of them, even her shift.

"Where—?" she swallowed. Her voice was hoarse, her throat as raw as her knee. "Who are you?" she tried again. She felt hot blood fill her cheeks, and panic formed a tight knot in her chest, and she tried again to remember what had happened, but her mind was blank. If he was—unclothed, and she was equally unclothed—

"What—" she began again, then swallowed the question

she couldn't frame. She hardly knew what to ask first, Where, Who, or What? Her mind was moving slowly, her thoughts as thick and rusty as her tongue.

"You're safe, lass," he said, and she wondered if she was. She stared at him. She'd seen men working in the summer sun, their shirts off, their bodies tanned, their muscles straining, but she'd never thought anything of it. This—he—was different. And she was as naked as he was.

An Excerpt from

RUNNING HOT
A Bad Boys Undercover Novella
by *HelenKay Dimon*

Ward Bennett and Tasha Gregory aren't on the
same team. But while hunting a dictator on the
run, these two must decide whether they can trust
one another—and their ability to stay professional.
Working together might just make everyone safer,
but getting cozy . . . might just get them killed.

"Take your clothes off."

He looked at her as if she'd lost her mind. "Excuse me?"

"You're attracted to me." Good Lord, now Tasha was waving her hands in the air. Once she realized it, she stopped. Curled her hands into balls at her sides. "I find you . . . fine."

Ward covered his mouth and produced a fake cough. She assumed it hid a smile. That was almost enough to make her rescind the offer.

"Really? That's all you can muster?" This time he did smile. "You think I'm fine?"

He was hot and tall and had a face that played in her head long after she closed her eyes each night. And that body. Long and lean, with the stalk of a predator. Ward was a man who protected and fought. She got the impression he wrestled demons that had to do with reconciling chivalry and decency with the work they performed.

The combination of all that made her wild with need. "Your clothes are still on."

"Are you saying you want to—"

Since he was saying the sentence so slowly—emphasizing, and halting after, each word—she finished it fast. "Shag."

Both eyebrows rose now. "Please tell me that's British for 'have sex.'"

"Yes."

He blew out a long, staggered breath. "Thank God, because right now my body is in a race to see what will explode first, my brain or my dick."

Uh? "Is that a compliment?"

"Believe it or not, yes." Two steps, and he was in front of her, his fingers playing with the small white button at the top of her slim tee. "So, are you talking about now or sometime in the future to celebrate ending Tigana?"

Both. "I need to work off this extra energy and get back in control." She was half-ready to rip off her clothes and throw him on the mattress.

Maybe he knew because he just stood there and stared at her, his gaze not leaving her face.

She stared back.

Just as he started to lower his head, a ripple moved through her. She shoved a hand against his shoulder. "Don't think that I always break protocol like this."

"I don't care if you do." He ripped his shirt out of his pants and whipped it over his head, revealing miles of tanned muscles and skin.

"You're taking off your clothes." Not the smartest thing she'd ever said, but it was out there and she couldn't snatch it back.

"You're the boss, remember?"

A shot of regret nearly knocked her over. Not at making the pass but at wanting him this much in the first place. Here and now, when her mind should be on the assignment, not on his chest.

She'd buried this part of herself for so long under a pile of work and professionalism that bringing it out now made her twitchy. "This isn't—"

His hands went to her arms, and he brushed those palms up and down, soothing her. "Do you want me?"

She couldn't lie. He had to feel it in the tremor shaking through her. "Yes."

"Then stop justifying not working this very second and enjoy. It won't make you less of a professional."

That was exactly what she needed to hear. "Okay."

His hands stopped at her elbows, and he dragged her in closer, until the heat of his body radiated against her. "You're a stunning woman, and we've been circling each other for days. Honestly, your ability to handle weapons only makes you hotter in my eyes."

The words spun through her. They felt so good. So right. "Not the way I would say it, but okay."

"You want me. I sure as hell want you. We need to lie low until it gets dark and we can hide our movements better." The corner of his mouth kicked up in a smile filled with promise. "And, for the record, there is nothing sexier than a woman who goes after what she wants."

He meant it. She knew it with every cell inside her.

Screw being safe.

An Excerpt from

SINFUL REWARDS 1
A Billionaires and Bikers Novella
by Cynthia Sax

Belinda "Bee" Carter is a good girl; at least, that's
what she tells herself. And a good girl deserves
a nice guy—just like the gorgeous and moody
billionaire Nicolas Rainer. Or so she thinks,
until she takes a look through her telescope
and sees a naked, tattooed man on the balcony
across the courtyard. He has been watching
her, and that makes him all the more enticing.
But when a mysterious and anonymous text
message dares her to do something bad, she
must decide if she is really the good girl she has
always claimed to be, or if she's willing to risk
everything for her secret fantasy of being watched.

An Avon Red Novella

I'd told Cyndi I'd never use it, that it was an instrument purchased by perverts to spy on their neighbors. She'd laughed and called me a prude, not knowing that I was one of those perverts, that I secretly yearned to watch and be watched, to care and be cared for.

If I'm cautious, and I'm always cautious, she'll never realize I used her telescope this morning. I swing the tube toward the bench and adjust the knob, bringing the mysterious object into focus.

It's a phone. Nicolas's phone. I bounce on the balls of my feet. This is a sign, another declaration from fate that we belong together. I'll return Nicolas's much-needed device to him. As a thank you, he'll invite me to dinner. We'll talk. He'll realize how perfect I am for him, fall in love with me, marry me.

Cyndi will find a fiancé also—everyone loves her—and we'll have a double wedding, as sisters of the heart often do. It'll be the first wedding my family has had in generations.

Everyone will watch us as we walk down the aisle. I'll wear a strapless white Vera Wang mermaid gown with organza and lace details, crystal and pearl embroidery accents, the bodice fitted, and the skirt hemmed for my shorter height. My hair will be swept up. My shoes—

Voices murmur outside the condo's door, the sound piercing my delightful daydream. I swing the telescope upward, not wanting to be caught using it. The snippets of conversation drift away.

I don't relax. If the telescope isn't positioned in the same way as it was last night, Cyndi will realize I've been using it. She'll tease me about being a fellow pervert, sharing the story, embellished for dramatic effect, with her stern, serious dad—or, worse, with Angel, that snobby friend of hers.

I'll die. It'll be worse than being the butt of jokes in high school because that ridicule was about my clothes and this will center on the part of my soul I've always kept hidden. It'll also be the truth, and I won't be able to deny it. I am a pervert.

I have to return the telescope to its original position. This is the only acceptable solution. I tap the metal tube.

Last night, my man-crazy roommate was giggling over the new guy in three-eleven north. The previous occupant was a gray-haired, bowtie-wearing tax auditor, his luxurious accommodations supplied by Nicolas. The most exciting thing he ever did was drink his tea on the balcony.

According to Cyndi, the new occupant is a delicious piece of man candy—tattooed, buff, and head-to-toe lickable. He was completing armcurls outside, and she enthusiastically counted his reps, oohing and aahing over his bulging biceps, calling to me to take a look.

I resisted that temptation, focusing on making macaroni and cheese for the two of us, the recipe snagged from the diner my mom works in. After we scarfed down dinner, Cyndi licking her plate clean, she left for the club and hasn't returned.

Three-eleven north is the mirror condo to ours. I

straighten the telescope. That position looks about right, but then, the imitation UGGs I bought in my second year of college looked about right also. The first time I wore the boots in the rain, the sheepskin fell apart, leaving me barefoot in Economics 201.

Unwilling to risk Cyndi's friendship on "about right," I gaze through the eyepiece. The view consists of rippling golden planes, almost like . . .

Tanned skin pulled over defined abs.

I blink. It can't be. I take another look. A perfect pearl of perspiration clings to a puckered scar. The drop elongates more and more, stretching, snapping. It trickles downward, navigating the swells and valleys of a man's honed torso.

No. I straighten. This is wrong. I shouldn't watch our sexy neighbor as he stands on his balcony. If anyone catches me . . .

Parts 1 – 6 available now!

An Excerpt from

RETURN TO CLAN SINCLAIR
A Clan Sinclair Novella
by Karen Ranney

When Ceana Sinclair Mead married the youngest
son of an Irish duke, she never dreamed that
seven years later her beloved Peter would die.
Her three brothers-in-law think she should
be grateful to remain a proper widow. After
three years of this, she's ready to scream. She
escapes to Scotland, only to discover she's so
much more than just the Widow Mead.

In Scotland, Ceana crosses paths with Bruce
Preston, an American tasked with a dangerous
mission by her brother, Macrath. Bruce is too
attractive for her peace of mind, but she still
finds him fascinating. Their one night together
is more wonderful than Ceana could have
imagined, and she has never felt more alive.

The darkness was nearly absolute, leaving her no choice but to stretch her hands out on either side of her, fingertips brushing against the stone walls. The incline was steep, further necessitating she take her time. Yet at the back of her mind was the last image she had of Carlton, his bright impish grin turning to horror as he glanced down.

The passage abruptly ended in a mushroom-shaped cavern. This was the grotto she'd heard so much about, with its flue in the middle and its broad, wide window looking out over the beach and the sea. She raced to the window, hopped up on the sill nature had created over thousands of years and leaned out.

A naked man reached up, grabbed Carlton as he fell. After he lowered the boy to the sand, he turned and smiled at her.

Carlton was racing across the beach, glancing back once or twice to see if he was indeed free. The rope made of sheets was hanging limply from his window.

The naked man was standing there with hands on his hips, staring at her in full frontal glory.

She hadn't seen many naked men, the last being her husband. The image in front of her now was so startling she couldn't help but stare. A smile was dawning on the stranger's full lips, one matched by his intent brown eyes. No, not quite brown, were they? They were like the finest Scottish whiskey touched with sunlight.

Her gaze danced down his strong and corded neck to broad shoulders etched with muscle. His chest was broad and muscled as well, tapering down to a slim waist and hips.

Even semiflaccid, his manhood was quite impressive.

The longer she watched, the more impressive it became.

What on earth was a naked man doing on Macrath's beach?

To her utter chagrin, the stranger turned and presented his backside to her, glancing over his shoulder to see if she approved of the sight.

She withdrew from the window, cheeks flaming. What on earth had she been doing? Who was she to gawk at a naked man as if she'd never before seen one?

Now that she knew Carlton was going to survive his escape, she should retreat immediately to the library.

"You'd better tell Alistair his brother's gotten loose again. Are you the new governess?"

She turned to find him standing in the doorway, still naked.

She pressed her fingers against the base of her throat and counseled herself to appear unaffected.

"I warn you, the imp escapes at any chance. You'll have your hands full there."

The look of fright on Carlton's face hadn't been fear of the distance to the beach, but the fact that he'd been caught.

She couldn't quite place the man's accent, but it wasn't Scottish. American, perhaps. What did she care where he came from? The problem was what he was doing here.

"I'm not a governess," she said. "I'm Macrath's sister, Ceana."

He bent and retrieved his shirt from a pile of clothes beside the door, taking his time with it. Shouldn't he have begun with his trousers instead?

"Who are you?" she asked, looking away as he began to don the rest of his clothing.

She'd had two children. She was well versed in matters of nature. She knew quite well what a man's body looked like. The fact that his struck her as singularly attractive was no doubt due to the fact she'd been a widow for three years.

"Well, Ceana Sinclair, is it all that important you know who I am?"

"It isn't Sinclair," she said. "It's Mead."

He tilted his head and studied her.

"Is Mr. Mead visiting along with you?"

She stared down at her dress of unremitting black. "I'm a widow," she said.

A shadow flitted over his face "Are you? Did Macrath know you were coming?"

"No," she said. "Does it matter? He's my brother. He's family. And why would you be wanting to know?"

He shrugged, finished buttoning his pants and began to don his shoes.

"Who are you?" she asked again.

"I'm a detective," he said. "My company was hired by your brother."

"Why?"

"Now that's something I'm most assuredly not going to tell you," he said. "It was nice meeting you, Mrs. Mead. I hope to see more of you before I leave."

And she hoped to see much, much less of him.

An Excerpt from

RETURN OF THE BAD GIRL
by Codi Gary

When Caroline Willis learns that her perfect
apartment has been double-booked—to a
dangerously hot bad boy—her bad-girl reputation
comes out in full force. But as close quarters
begin to ignite the sizzling chemistry between
them, she's left wondering: Bad boy plus bad
girl equals nothing but trouble . . . right?

"I feel like you keep looking for something more to me, but what you know about me is it. There's no 'deep down,' no mistaking my true character. I am bad news." He waited, listening for the tap of her retreating feet or the slam of the door, but only silence met his ears, then the soft sound of shoes on the cement floor—getting closer to him instead of farther away.

Fingers trailed feather-light touches over his lower back. "This scar on your back—is that from the accident?"

Her caress made his skin tingle as he shook his head. "I was knocked down by one of my mother's boyfriends and landed on a glass table."

"What about here?" Her hand had moved onto his right shoulder.

"It was a tattoo I had removed. In prison, you're safer if you belong, so—"

"I understand," she said, cutting him off. Had she heard the pain in his voice, or did she really understand?

He turned around before she could point out any more scars. "What are you doing?"

She looked him in the eye and touched the side of his neck, where his tattoo began, spreading all the way down past his shoulder and over his chest. "You say you're damaged. That you're bad news and won't ever change."

"Yeah?"

To his surprise, she dropped her hand to his and brought it up to her collarbone, where his finger felt a rough, puckered line.

"This is a knife wound—just a scratch, really—that I got from a man who used to come see me dance at the strip club. He was constantly asking me out, and I always let him down easy. But one night, after I'd had a shitty day, I told him I would never go out with an old, ugly fuck like him. He was waiting by my car when I got off work."

His rage blazed at this phantom from her past. "What happened?"

"I pulled a move I'd learned from one of the bouncers. Even though he still cut me, I was able to pick up a handful of gravel and throw it in his face. I made it to the front door of the club, and he took off. They arrested him on assault charges, and it turned out he had an outstanding warrant. I never saw him again."

Caroline pulled him closer, lifting her arm for him to see a jagged scar along her forearm. "This is from a broken beer bottle I got sliced with when a woman came into my bar in San Antonio, looking for her husband. She didn't take it well when she found out he had a girlfriend on the side, and when I stepped in to stop her from attacking him, she sliced me."

He couldn't stop his hand from sliding up over her soft skin until it rested on the back of her neck, his fingers pressing into her flesh until she tilted her chin up to meet his gaze.

"What's your point with all the show-and-tell, Caroline?"

She reached out and smoothed his chest with her hand. "I don't care how damaged you are, because I am just as broken, maybe more so."

Her words tore at him, twisting him up inside as his other hand cupped the back of her head. "You don't want to go here with me, princess. I'm only going to break your heart."

The laugh that passed those beautiful lips was bitter and sad. "Trust me, my heart was shattered long before I ever met you."

Gabe wanted her, wanted to believe that he could find comfort in her body without the complications that would inevitably come, but he'd seen her heart firsthand. She had one. It might be wrapped up in a mile-thick layer of cowhide, but a part of Caroline Willis was still open to new emotions. New love.

And he wasn't.

But he wanted to kiss her anyway.

He dropped his head until his lips hovered above hers, and he watched as they parted when he came closer. Her hot breath teased his mouth, and he couldn't stop while she was warm and willing. He might not get another chance to taste her, and while a better man would have walked away, he wasn't that guy.